NIGHTWALKER 6

NIGHTWALKER 6
WRITTEN BY CRAIG MARTELLE, CREATED BY

FRANK RODERUS

DISRUPTIVE IMAGINATION

NIGHTWALKER 6 TEAM

Thanks to our Beta Readers

Micky Cocker, Dr. Jim Caplan, Kelly O'Donnell, and John
Ashmore

Thanks to our JIT Readers

Micky Cocker
Kelly O'Donnell
Jeff Goode
Misty Roa
John Ashmore
Larry Omans

Editor
Lynne Stiegler

CHAPTER ONE

B uddy, the big wolf/German Shepherd mix, was upside-down in the back seat of the truck, snoring loudly. Jim Wolfe removed his goggles, bringing the dog into focus.

Sunlight caused Wolfe pain. His transformation was the result of spending two years underground after the bombs fell. When he emerged, he was able to see in the dark, and he was stronger—unnaturally so. His hair had turned white, and he could sense radiation.

His body had adapted to the new world, even if he did not know it at the time. Wolfe pulled the handle and pushed the door open, sliding out without making a sound. The young girl who traveled with him, Jennifer, was curled into a ball in the front seat, sheltering herself from the outside as an armadillo might. He watched her to see if she would stir before carefully closing the truck door behind him.

The fog had settled, making it dangerous to drive any farther. Seeing in the dark wasn't the same as seeing through fog.

Wolfe took stock of his surroundings, pacing around the

truck before picking the direction they had been traveling and heading into the mist.

He listened as he walked, his blowgun in one hand and his bow in the other. He did not want to eat the food the good people of Ashland had provided, not if he didn't have to.

A splash and swish. Brush moving when the air was still. On both sides of the road, water filled the ditches, extending as far as Wolfe could see. At the edge of his sight, a movement drew his attention. He stepped toward it, dropping his copper-tube blowgun and gripping his bow. With his free hand, he pulled an arrow from the quiver over his shoulder— one of his lesser arrows. He only had two more that had been made before the war. The rest had wood shafts and bird-feather fletching and were the best that could be made without technology.

Good enough when hunting, but there was always the risk that they would not fly true. He trusted his strength and speed should an animal attack. He had yet to meet his match and did not expect to do so in the expanding swamps of the Arkansas-Louisiana border area.

A splash jerked his attention to the left side of the road, and he heard a sound to the right. He crouched, using his peripheral vision to scan for movement. The gator burst out of the water, running straight for him. Wolfe fell sideways, launching the arrow high into the fog. He rolled and came back to his feet.

The gator was on him. He jumped as the jaws opened, then snapped closed on the empty space where he had been. It continued for a few steps before its legs brought it to a halt. Wolfe came down with one leg on the thing's back while it was trying to turn around and he stumbled and fell to the side. The gator turned toward him, its head twisting while it tried to get its body in position to charge again.

Wolfe grabbed a back leg and pulled, jerking the gator's head away.

Wolfe jumped to his feet, hanging on to the leg, lifting the back half of the gator off the ground as he maneuvered away from its snapping jaws. He let go to wrap both hands around the gator's tail. He pulled it off the ground and started to spin it around. He turned faster and faster as he staggered toward the side of the road. With a final lunge and twist, he accelerated the gator's neck into a road sign's metal post.

He hoped it would cut the creature's head off, but it didn't. It barely dented the tough hide, but it was enough to stun the gator. Wolfe crawled to its head, straddling the swamp-stinking beast, then wrapped an arm under its throat and tried to choke it to death.

The best-laid plans. Gators did not like being choked. When it came to, it started to thrash and twist, nearly breaking free of Wolfe's grip. Wolfe worked his way to his feet, arched his back, and pulled the gator over him as he drove the creature's snout into the pavement. Wolfe continued his wrestling move, rolling back on top. He pinned it to the ground while he removed his belt knife and jammed it hilt-deep into the skull.

With a last contortion and twist, the creature died.

Wolfe removed his knife, and for good measure, cut the gator's throat.

A vicious growl shot his heart into his throat. Wolfe dove across the gator, turned, and crouched with his knife ready. Buddy snapped and slavered at the dead gator. Jennifer stood next to him. Wolfe flopped to the ground, looking left and right to make sure they were safe before he relaxed.

"What is it, Mister Wolfe?" Jennifer asked, the innocence of her question catching him off-guard. Buddy sniffed the body and started barking again. The young girl petted him to calm him down.

"That is an alligator, Miss Jennifer. We have a lot of them down home in Florida, but I never thought they would be this far north." Wolfe did not add, *I am afraid this is not going to make our journey any easier.*

"Can we eat him?" She wrinkled her nose at the thought.

"Now that, Miss Jennifer, is a treat you do not want to miss. The tail tastes like chicken." Wolfe seized the creature by the tail and gestured for them to return to the truck, where their midnight snack would be carved up and cooked.

CHAPTER TWO

Jim Wolfe crawled into the back of the truck and slept like a dead man. He was used to sleeping with his goggles on because he usually slept during the daytime. When the sun started burning off the fog, he started awake, wincing, and pinched his eyes closed until he was able to cover them. He scratched his head as he sat up. Jennifer and Buddy were inside the truck and still sleeping. They would wake up soon enough when it got warm.

The remainder of the gator's tail was wrapped in a cloth bag on top of the cab. A crow pecked at it.

"Go on now!" Wolfe shooed the bird away. "There is plenty over there." He pointed to where he'd cleaned the creature during the night, but there was nothing there. "What is big enough to take what was left of that gator?"

He knew the answer but did not want to say it aloud. He pulled the tail into the truck bed and carefully looked around the area now that he could see. The road continued into the distance, raised above the water on either side.

"At least that is in our favor. Have you always been a swamp?" he asked the murky waters. He could not remember ever having traveled these roads. They were country highways, not the interstate. Those high-speed, twin-lane roads traveled to and through areas that had been on the receiving end of the bombs and were hot zones now. The only way left for Wolfe to travel was on side- and backroads.

He checked the ground for gators before jumping down. When he hit the earth, something shot out from under the truck, skimmed across the ground, and launched itself into the water. He saw that it was a four-foot gator, a relative baby, resting in the shade. Wolfe wondered if he and his fellows had made short work of the carcass. It was probably better not to know.

He climbed into the truck and turned the key. The engine turned over slowly before catching and belching a cloud of blue smoke out the tailpipe. It grumbled and bucked before settling into the rattling purr of a truck with worn rings.

Wolfe checked the disc, turned up Hank Williams, and put it in gear. The truck rolled forward easily and cruised easily at twenty-five miles per hour. The gas gauge was between a quarter of a tank and empty. Wolfe nudged the truck up to forty-five for the best gas mileage, taking care to watch as far ahead as possible.

He would do what he had to to get back to Lurleen and JoJo, but he much preferred driving to walking. In two days, they had covered more territory than the three months prior. They were making good time and doing it in comfort.

But when they ran out of gas—and he did not expect to find more—they would be back to walking. The longer he could delay that eventuality, the happier he would be.

In the end, it was not the gas that held them back, it was the wreckage strewn across the road. Apparently, two semis had collided and left the entire one hundred and sixty thousand pounds they had been carrying in a single charred pile. Wolfe stopped the truck a hundred yards short and watched.

"What are we waiting for?" The young girl, always practical, was readying her backpack, stuffing in the last of their prepared food. She dutifully checked around her seat to make sure she did not leave anything behind.

"I want to be sure. Maybe you and Buddy can wait here while I check it out," Wolfe suggested. She nodded, tight-lipped. He said no other words, simply got out of the truck and motioned for her to lock the doors before he left. He took only his rifle. The only predator he expected to find was man.

CHAPTER THREE

Wolfe approached the wreck. He carried his AR-15 with a fully-loaded magazine inserted and a round in the chamber. He had taken the opportunity at the armory in Ashland to fill his pack and magazines, and now he had enough ammunition to fight a war. Most likely, knowing himself, he would trade it, or give it away to those in need.

People were struggling in the new world, good people like the citizens of Ashland, who only needed a chance to throw off the burden of those who used their power for evil. Wolfe figured he would run into that again and again—strongmen filling the government void. And sometimes they were not even men, like the creature who led Paradise. He was happy that she was no more. He wondered how the people had fared after he left.

Traded one tyrant for another, probably. It depressed him to think about it, but only for a moment. He had done all he was capable of doing, and he was committed to carrying that torch. If he saw injustice, he would address it. Lurleen and JoJo would understand. He felt they would think less of him if he did not help those in need.

He wrapped those thoughts around him like a warm blanket. He could only imagine what doing right by his family meant. It had been so long since he had seen them that he was starting to forget little details. What did Lurleen listen to on the radio? Country, but she would flip over to the news at lunchtime. What was that station? It would not come to him.

But he remembered every detail of her face, her smile, and the sparkle in her eyes. He blinked away the moisture that threatened his eyes and focused on the two semi-trucks in front of him.

He slung his rifle when he found no signs of recent activity. The wreckage had been abandoned a long time ago. The heavily-rusted vehicles stood as a monument to the time of turmoil. Trails led through the wreckage, as if both people and animals had cleared a path to get from one side to the other. He worked his way to the other side, to find the open road leading into the distance.

If only he could clear enough space to get by. The water and muck in the ditches were less than a swamp, and from what he could see, there were no tracks or indications that gators were nearby.

He returned to the truck, flashing the okay sign. Jennifer opened the door to let Buddy out. The big dog ran down the road to sniff the wreckage. He raised his leg to mark his spot.

Jennifer called him, and he happily ran back to her. She hoisted her backpack over her shoulders and shrugged it into place.

"We might not be walking just yet, Miss Jennifer," Wolfe told her. He waved her to the side as he carefully turned the truck around and backed up to the overturned trailer of one rig. The vehicles had already been cleaned out, scavenged for whatever they contained. At the back of the big rig's cab, he wrapped a bundle of cables around his hand and pulled. It jerked toward him as it came free, but stopped when it hit another snag. Wolfe braced himself and pulled harder, pushing with his legs until a final yank broke it free. He lost his balance and stumbled, falling to the pavement. He brushed himself off and got back to work.

Wolfe tied one end around a bracket in the middle of the forward section of the trailer bed. He tied the other end to the truck's hitch, then climbed in and eased the truck forward to take the slack out of his ad hoc tow cable. Wolfe gave it some gas, but nothing moved. He jammed the pedal down, barking the rear wheels as they lost traction. There was nothing to lose. Either they were able to move the trailer far enough to create a gap through which they could drive or they walked.

He jammed the pedal down and the truck accelerated, throwing Wolfe forward when it hit the end of the cable and jerked. The engine screamed as it started to move the mass. Wolfe bounced as he encouraged the truck to keep pulling, and it worked its way forward ten more feet before something popped in the engine compartment and steam funneled out. He put it in Park and shut down the engine.

Wolfe looked at the truck without opening the hood.

"Is it broke?" Jennifer asked. Buddy started to bark at the hissing coming from behind the grill.

"Maybe a little," Wolfe replied. "But I might be able to fix it. We have some tools and a pile of spare parts." He pointed at the semis. "Something might work to get us back on the road. We will see once the radiator cools down."

When the steam stopped, Wolfe popped the hood so he could see which hose had failed. It was the coolant return line, the big hose with the hottest fluid. All he had to do was fix it well enough to hold water for another hundred miles, maybe less. They did not have a lot of gas left. If the big rigs had any remaining, it would have been diesel. Save five to ten days' walking time to get another hundred miles behind them.

As soon as he could work on it, he would. In the meantime, there were other things they could do to pass the time productively.

"I say we cook up the last of the gator, and then you learn how to use the blowgun."

CHAPTER FOUR

Wolfe wanted Jennifer to be a natural, but she hesitated too long. Still targets like a small rock set in the distance, she could hit every time. But something like a frog? She waited and aimed and adjusted and waited some more before gulping a big breath of air with so much noise that it made the frog jump.

"You have plenty of air."

"I am sorry, Mister Wolfe." She did not continue her train of thought.

"Keep at it. One after another until you are comfortable," Wolfe encouraged the young girl. She was not as tall as she could have been for her age—twelve years old, but barely over four feet. She could have passed for younger, and people often thought she was. It did not matter to her or Wolfe. She ate well and was healthy. He rested his hand on his adopted daughter's shoulder.

She sent pellet after pellet into a target leaning against the truck. When she had emptied the small pouch, she skipped away to start picking them up. Wolfe moved to the side of the road and kicked dirt over their fire.

"Can you start a fire without a lighter?" he asked.

"Of course," she replied, occupied with refilling her pouch. She found the small bearings from wherever they'd stopped rolling. He was amazed by her eyesight. With his welding goggles on in the daylight, he could see without pain, but things were a shade hazy because the welding goggles were impossible to keep clean and grit-free. They had been through the war.

Or at least, a number of battles.

Jennifer sat down again and started pinging away at the target. She could hit an area smaller and more consistently than Wolfe, but not nearly as hard. She might not have enough power to kill a bird. Then again, they had thin skulls.

"Wait," he told her. He crawled into the cab through the crushed windshield and dug around the glove compartment. He found an old manual, half-torn and a little soggy. "Here."

Wolfe put two pages from the manual in front of her target.

"Now hit it."

Her first five attempts bounced off. She huffed and glared at the paper.

Wolfe watched the determination creep onto her features. Her lips turned white while she clenched her jaw. She started taking deeper and deeper breaths. When she had the biggest she could hold, Jennifer let fly, sending the pellet wide. Her shoulders slumped with her failure. Wolfe smiled at her.

"You are close to perfect. Every time we stop, I want you to practice. Both of us hunting are better than one. It will keep us from starving."

"Three of us," she corrected, nodding toward the truck. Buddy was curled up in the shade under the rear bumper. "I will do my share, Mister Wolfe. I do not want to be a burden…" Her voice trailed off.

Wolfe knew where her mind had gone. She was back in

the cabin with her parents. She frowned and blinked to keep the tears from coming.

"You had nothing to do with all that. Things happened that no one could control. Your parents were good people. You think kindly about them, Miss Jennifer."

She nodded while sniffling.

Wolfe decided it was time to fix the truck. Duct tape would have worked well enough, but he did not have any. He crawled under the front end, avoiding the puddle of water with a touch of anti-freeze. Spring clamps held the hose in place, and he had it off in seconds. The outside rubber flaked away under his fingers.

Grumbling, he took the hose to the first semi's engine compartment. He found nothing in good enough shape or small enough. The second truck, a Peterbilt, was more fruitful. He found a silicon hose that had been protected from the elements. It was limber but a little too big. He tested the original hose to see if it would fit inside the better hose.

He returned to the truck, where he sliced off two one-inch sections of the original hose. He used those as spacers and gaskets. He stretched the spring clamps as far as they would go before fitting the gasket and new hose. He sealed the end and looked for gaps, then manhandled the new hose to twist it into place on the engine block, leaving a kink in the middle. Nothing he did changed that. He clamped the second connection tightly and crawled out.

"One hundred miles," he told the truck. "All we need is a hundred miles out of you, and we will be much obliged."

Using a rag he found under the truck seat as a filter, Wolfe and Jennifer used their canteens to get water from the ditches to fill the radiator. When it was done, he twisted the radiator cap into place and brushed off his hands.

"We might have to take a little bit of a run at it," he said, eyeing the narrow gap. They climbed in, and the truck slowly turned over until it started. It belched blue smoke before settling in. Wolfe turned it around and eased it toward the opening. Metal screeched as the truck touched the trailer on one side and the semi's roof on the other. He backed out.

"Roll the window down and get in the back with Buddy. Hold him down." Wolfe looked at the gap as if it were an enemy that needed to be defeated. "One hundred miles starts here."

Jennifer did as she was asked, crawling over the console and into the back. She forced the big dog to the floor, where she covered him with her body. He whimpered in protest but only fought weakly. Wolfe's rifle, bow, and gear were behind his seat, and the dog and the young girl filled the rest of the space.

Wolfe gunned the engine with his right foot on the gas pedal and his left on the brake. He lifted his left and the truck raced into the gap, impacting the wreckage with a horrible rending of metal and jerking to a halt. The rusted remains of the semis had wedged into both driver and passenger door frames. Wolfe tried to back up but could not. They were trapped.

"Can you get out?" Wolfe asked. Jennifer looked out one window and then the other.

"I cannot," she finally answered.

"I need to come back there," Wolfe told her. Buddy was already standing on the back seat, refusing to return to the floor. His hackles were up as he tried to figure out what was happening.

"Come on, Buddy. Give Mister Wolfe some space." She pulled the big beast to the side, trying to look hopeful that it was enough.

Wolfe contorted his body until he was crouched over the console and twisted sideways between the two front seats.

He kicked out, driving the back window into the bed of the truck, surprised it had come out in one piece.

"Our way out." He gestured for Jennifer to climb through, and she made quick and easy work of it. Buddy pranced around the back seat, unwilling to try to fit through the space. Wolfe had had enough of it. He fought with the dog while trying to climb into the back seat. Once he forced Buddy's head and front legs through, the rest followed. When the way was clear, Wolfe handed their gear through the opening, making sure there was nothing left behind before he squeezed his body through.

With a final sigh, he led the way through the wreckage and onto the clear road beyond.

Sometimes the world conspired against you, no matter how hard you tried to bend it to your will.

CHAPTER FIVE

They spent the rest of that day and the next walking in silence. As Wolfe had asked, Jennifer practiced with her blowgun.

On the third day, she bagged her first bird. Wolfe cooked it in their one pot with water and leeks to make a weak soup. Buddy caught himself a fish in a roadside stream, but despite Wolfe's best efforts, he could not catch one to add to the pot.

Once they finished eating, Jennifer cleaned the pot in the stream. The water ran crystal clear, the sound of its passing leaving a certain calm in its wake. Birds sang from the trees overhead.

Jennifer dropped another bird, a big one.

Wolfe did not caution her about killing too many. Tomorrow they would move on, but today, they were still hungry. He nodded to her as she started to clean her kill using a small pocketknife.

He heard a rustle in the bushes, a sound that was different from the other sounds. Wolfe's head snapped around, and he brought the rifle barrel up to follow his line of sight. He studied the bushes, still moving despite a lack of wind.

"Over here, Miss Jennifer," Wolfe whispered. She hurried toward him, calling to Buddy as she went. A small, furry black head appeared, looking up at the strangers before falling into the swollen and fast-moving stream. A second bear cub followed the first into the water. The mother roared her displeasure as she tore out half the bushes to splash in after the mischievous youths. She snapped her jaws at the humans before swimming downstream to rescue her offspring.

Wolfe watched the bear through the rifle sights, following her as she swam away. Jennifer put her hand on his arm and pulled the barrel down.

"I will get better, so we do not have to kill a mother or her babies."

"I would not, Miss Jennifer. She was safe as long as she stayed over there."

Jennifer started to laugh. "The cubs fell in the water."

"And Mom was not happy about that," Wolfe added with a smile. "It is a universal thing. My Lurleen…" Wolfe hung his head. "I hope you get to meet her someday, and your little brother JoJo."

"We will." The young girl wrapped her arms around Wolfe and hugged him. He patted her back as he watched the stream. The soft whisper of the running water and the innocence of bird song returned. "I can sleep now, and we will walk at night, Mister Wolfe, to make it easier on you."

"I appreciate that, little lady, but it is not necessary. We will be okay. We'll walk now and rest later."

Jennifer nodded, picked up her pack, and got ready to go.

Wolfe checked his bow, kicking himself for not cutting a pipe from the semi to use as a backup blowgun. Maybe he didn't need to. The copper tubing from a house worked best. He would stick to that.

He thumbed through the magazines for his rifle,

bouncing them against his hand to make sure the rounds within were seated primer-first. It was a trick the old veteran had shown him in Ashland to reduce the chance of a bullet hanging up, resulting in a misfeed and jamming the rifle. If he was aiming to shoot something, he could not risk the rifle not firing.

Wolfe put the magazines back into his pack and carried the rifle loosely in his hands. He could not put his finger on why he was delaying, but felt like he was dragging his feet. Jennifer looked impatient, and Buddy had already started ahead.

"We are not getting closer by standing here," he said more to himself than the girl. She started, and he caught up quickly, to walk side by side as they usually did. She tried to increase her stride to walk faster, but she still took almost twice as many steps as Wolfe.

And always without complaint. Buddy dove into the brush ahead and yelped in pain. Wolfe and Jennifer started to run.

CHAPTER SIX

Wolfe leaped over the bush, landing clean on the other side, to find a raccoon engaged in mortal combat with the big dog. Buddy had recovered his senses and snapped at the raccoon, which stood on its hind legs, parrying with its paws as it tried to bite the dog's nose a second time. Blood and a tear marked a future scar that would mar Buddy's nose.

Wolfe thought about the ways he could kill the raccoon and decided quickest was best. He stepped aside and fired once from a range of one foot, and the back half of the raccoon's head disappeared in a red and white mist. The coon fell over, flopped twice, and stilled. Jennifer wrapped herself around the big dog to keep him from running off with their kill.

"What does it taste like?" Jennifer grunted as she continued to struggle with her friend. Wolfe picked the raccoon up by the tail and held it high, out of the dog's reach.

"Settle down. You will get your share when the time is right," Wolfe told Buddy. "I don't rightly know. I expect it will be greasy, but if we rinse it well, we could have ourselves a good meal."

Wolfe was right. Between a choice of thinly watered soup with an ounce or two of a small finch or raccoon roasted on a spit, Wolfe knew exactly what he preferred. They were not disappointed with the result. They finally had a meal where they could eat their fill. Buddy dined on the less savory bits but seemed happy with his lot in life, despite the scab across his nose.

The big dog's ears perked up, and he started to growl. Jennifer froze since he was looking at something behind her. Wolfe stood, motioning for her stay down.

A man and a woman pushed through the low bushes and stood there, not making eye contact. The man had a filthy old hat that he held with both hands. His skin was sucked tight against his bones, with little muscle in between. The woman looked the same. Wolfe could not guess their ages. These two had lived a hard life and were starving.

"We would be honored if you joined us," Wolfe offered.

"I-I-I don't know what to say, Mister," the man stammered.

"Call me Jim." Wolfe moved aside to give the people room. Jennifer wrapped her hand in the dog's neck fur to calm him down. He settled quickly when Jennifer moved off the log to give them room to sit. They looked hungrily at the raccoon. Wolfe cleaned his knife off in the fire and handed it over hilt-first. "Where did you come from?"

"We live over yonder in a shack on the edge of a lake, but we have lost most everything. The storms were bad this season, and the house flooded. Almost took us with it. Mary Lou and I barely escaped with our lives. The water drained out, but nothing was left. We are pretty far out here. We have not been able to recover anything to help us hunt or fish. We have had to live off scavenging these past two months."

"You seen the rain, Mister Jim?" the woman, Mary Lou, asked.

He shook his head. "We were out west." Jennifer cleaned her pocketknife and offered it to the woman.

"Please." Wolfe gestured toward the remainder of the raccoon. He almost felt guilty about having eaten the choicest meats first. Almost. He'd had no idea they were going to have to share with anyone other than the dog, and that beast would eat anything. He made sure Jennifer got the best of it, despite her efforts to give them to him. Keep up his strength, she had said almost as if she were becoming his guardian, instead of the other way around.

The two started tentatively, but then ravaged the remainder. A twenty-pound raccoon had fed four people and a big dog, but there was nothing left over.

"Can you tell me if there are any FEDCOMs in the area?" Wolfe asked.

"Who?" The man's question gave him the answer.

"They were the folks who took over the government after there was no government. After the bombs fell."

The man finished chewing and swallowed. "Bombs? Is that what happened? There was too much madness out on the road, so we stayed away. No one came to our place. And then one day, there was no one left. Our truck was dead, so we walked as far as we could, but there was nobody. We were out here all alone. That was fine, kinda how we liked it, but then we could not go to town for everything. We've been doing with what we could grow, hunt, or catch for the past few years. Until the floods, that is. Now we got nothin'."

"There is no United States left. There are Red Zones, Clear Areas, and Federal Command. Red Zones still have some radioactivity, but not too much. The Clear Areas are usually infested with soldiers from FEDCOM. The soldiers are a bunch of no-good thugs."

FRANK RODERUS

The man and woman nodded slowly, transfixed by Wolfe's words. They stared at the welding goggles on his face.

"The bombs. Damaged my eyes," he said before they could ask.

"Not our issue, Mister. We are sorry for intruding, but…" The woman let her question trail off.

Jennifer looked at Wolfe, her big eyes appealing.

"Do you want to come with us?" Wolfe asked, not turning to the couple but holding Jennifer's gaze. She smiled and nodded.

He felt like he should have been more assertive, but these people were going to die without his help. Dirt-poor would have been a step up.

"Are you serious?" The two held hands, eyes brightening. "We promise we will not be a burden. Don't we, Billy Ray?"

He nodded vigorously.

Wolfe contemplated his future. They would slow him down. Their shoes had holes so big he wondered why they did not go barefoot. They were in no shape to walk twenty-five miles a day. Then again, he only had to get them to the next settlement.

CHAPTER SEVEN

Billy Ray and Mary Lou returned to their shack, promising they would be back at first light. Wolfe made sure they knew he would leave without them if they were late.

Wolfe put on his goggles before he started the fire to heat up a tin of water for a cup of coffee. It had become a guilty pleasure because of the instant packets they had acquired from FEDCOM storage at the compound. The townsfolk had wanted him to have them. He paced himself, keeping it to one cup a day. Jennifer knew to leave him to his thoughts while he savored the brew.

She led Buddy into the brush to take care of business while Wolfe eased into the morning. He'd been on the road for so long that he could leave in ten seconds or ten minutes. He preferred working up to it since he found it hard to take that first step each day. The closer he got to Florida, the more he hesitated.

The more he found himself leaning on Jennifer. What if she was the only family he had left?

He already treated her that way, protecting her as much as she would allow.

If his wife and son lived, he would find them. If they didn't, he would be firm in his belief that they had gone quickly. There was no in-between, not in his mind. But until he was sure, his purpose was to get home, helping as many people as he could along the way.

Always remaining on the road home.

When Jennifer returned, Billy Ray and Mary Lou were with her.

Wolfe nodded to them. "Have you seen any gators?" Wolfe asked.

The woman's smile disappeared, and the man scowled. "They started showing up about a year ago, and they came in droves."

"Do you know why?" Wolfe pressed.

Billy Ray continued. "I think the Mississippi Delta flooded and sent the swamps north. The gators had nowhere to go. They are not open-water creatures."

"We will just have to steer clear of the water, then," Wolfe declared matter-of-factly. "Shall we?"

Wolfe did not wait. He wrapped an arm around Jennifer's shoulders on top of her pack, and they headed down the road at a good clip. Billy Ray and Mary Lou did their best to keep up, but one meal did not give them enough strength. They soon started to fall back.

"Keep going. We will catch up," Billy Ray offered.

"No." Wolfe's hair was growing out, and the roots were white. When he shook his head, it looked like silver minnows flashing through muddy water. "I think it's better if we stay in a group. Just in case."

"Mister Wolfe will protect you. It is what he does," Jennifer clarified. "You should feel safe."

They continued at a slower and slower pace until they

were barely crawling. Jennifer bagged a couple of small birds on the way, and Wolfe beamed with pride.

It was not enough food for four people. He took out his bow and arrow and told them to stop and start setting up camp, even though it was only early afternoon. Wolfe needed them to rebuild their strength before he could push them any harder. He estimated that they had only covered ten miles that day.

"How far have you walked after the bombs?"

"No farther than half this." Billy Ray replied. "But we drove this way twice a week before our truck died."

Wolfe had the map Bessie had given him. It did not have enough detail to be of much use, but it told him he was on the right roads and going in the right direction. They were on the south side of a river heading toward the Ozark National Forest. He was staying as far away from big cities and military bases as he could to avoid the radiation and FEDCOM. He knew which was more deadly. At least he could feel the radiation before it hurt him.

The terrain started to change. There was plenty of swamp, but tree-covered hills lined the view to the south.

"The Ouachita Forest." Billy Ray pointed to the trees before turning back to wave at the fast-moving body of water beyond the flooded fields to the north. "And that used to be the Arkansas River."

"Used to be?" Wolfe did not think rivers changed.

"It does not look anything like what I grew up with. It's not the Arkansas I know."

Wolfe studied the river briefly, the water highway the gators had traveled and were probably still infesting. "We will need to go around Little Rock. Do you know a way?"

"Been a while since I been to Little Rock. We do not like big cities."

Wolfe pulled out his map. He figured they were following

state highway 154 and it would turn into 113, but all roads led to Little Rock.

"Looks like we might have to go through the city. We can do that at night. I will guide us."

"Are you sure you can see all right?" Mary Lou asked.

"I see better at night." Wolfe left it at that. Jennifer removed her pack and started gathering dry wood. Their guests were able to sit down. They had moved as much as they could for the day. Wolfe felt sorry for them. He wondered why he had been given the gift of great strength and not hardworking folks like this couple.

Maybe it was to protect people like this and youth like Jennifer.

"I am going to find us something to eat," Wolfe declared before setting off at a slow run, putting distance between himself and the camp. When he could, he turned south and headed for the hills. With any luck, he'd run across bigger game like deer, or maybe a wild boar. Get more than a single meal's worth of meat.

As he forced his way through the heavy brush alongside the road, he saw what he'd hoped for—pig tracks. Looked like a big number of animals. Wolfe kept his bow over his pack, opting for the rifle. His entire focus was on following their potential dinner. Finally, his luck was improving.

CHAPTER EIGHT

The drove of pigs headed from one pit to the next in the general direction of the forested hillside. He expected they would turn and stick to the lowlands, so he stalked rather than chased, rifle up and ready in case he needed to take a shot. His thumb rested gently on the selection lever to flip the weapon off safe. His trigger finger rested outside the trigger guard as an added precaution. He knew how to handle a weapon, even though he had not been formally trained. He'd paid attention when people talked and watched what they did.

And that was why he trusted Billy Ray and Mary Lou. As long as Buddy was by Jennifer's side, she was safe if Wolfe was wrong. But he was not. He had started to read people better, looking at them with a more skeptical eye.

Buddy would have been a good addition to the hunt, but Wolfe did not have time to go back for the dog. Wolfe pressed on, tracking, watching, listening. He started to jog, wondering if the scent had run cold, but the tracks were fresh and sharp in the dirt, just like his.

He stopped and stood up straight. He was upwind. Wolfe

sprinted up the hillside to the ridge and kept running, parallel to the drove. He ran as fast as he could for at least a mile before drifting down the hill and slowing. He checked the undergrowth and dirt beneath. No sign of the drove's passage.

The strong odor of the pigs finally reached him, now that he was downwind. They were close. He cocked an ear; grunts and snorts sounded in the distance. Wolfe picked the best vantage point over open ground between him and the drove, then leaned around a tree, rifle barrel braced, and waited.

The first pig ran two steps into the open and froze. Others appeared behind it, forcing their way through the brush. Wolfe grinned. It had been a while since he'd had fresh meat that wasn't wild and greasy. Miss Bessie was a great cook, but there was something to fresh livestock cooked over an open fire.

The hogs looked like they had escaped from a farm, having pinkish skin without the tusks of a wild boar. He took aim, trying to pick a mid-sized animal, but stopped when a massive beast ripped a small tree out of the ground as it rushed into the opening, running like an Australian Shepherd corralling the herd. This boar had tusks, and it made Wolfe rethink his guess. Maybe wild boars had mixed with the domestic livestock to create this drove.

As the boar forced the pigs back into the brush, Wolfe decided he had to take the shot, even if it wasn't the best. He aimed and fired at the first hog that turned sideways. With the shot, the stampede started, the big beast racing after the others, leaving the dead animal behind. Wolfe listened for a moment, and then slung his rifle and pulled his knife. He walked across the opening, counting fifty paces to his target. It was one of the easier shots he had taken. Still, he hunted only for food.

There was no sport in this. After making sure the pig was

dead, he made the first cut to gut it and make it easier to carry. Plus he had no wish to leave a pile of refuse near their camp. Nothing would draw gators more quickly.

The boar stormed from the brush, making a beeline for Wolfe, who was unbalanced on his knees. He tried to lunge aside, but the boar was on him too quickly. He rolled backward, reaching for the tusks to keep them from driving into his body. He pushed the slavering jaws away from him as the heavy creature danced and skittered, trying to get free from Wolfe's iron grip.

Wolfe had no leverage. Every time he tried to twist the head to flop the beast on its side, it pulled him off balance. He struggled on his knees, unable to rise. The standoff lasted just shy of forever in Wolfe's mind. His rifle clattered off the bow across his back. The knife was lost near the dead pig. Hand to tusk, they fought, neither gaining an advantage over the other.

Despite Wolfe's immense strength, his arms started to tire. He was holding them out where he had little leverage, and the muscles on his arms bulged with the effort. Wolfe leaned forward to find purchase with his toes. The boar pulled back—only an inch, but it was enough. Wolfe pushed forward, his body straightened, and he came upright. He growled into the boar's face, its beady eyes flaring in its hatred.

Wolfe tried to get around the thing's head, but it moved with him, trying to use its superior bodyweight to its advantage. A new dance began. Wolfe kept his feet moving, darting glances to make sure that none of the others from the drove were coming in from behind. He heard the snorts over the grunts of the boar in his face. He yanked the head sideways to put the beast between him and where he'd last seen the others.

Sure enough, they were there, coming back slowly and

watching the fight. Wolfe pushed and then pulled the boar toward him, unbalancing the creature as it fought him. He rolled to his back, and with a mighty heave, pulled the boar over him. Using his legs, he lifted the boar into the air. Wolfe hung onto the tusks, twisting as the boar landed on its back. With a final lunge, he was over the boar's throat and able to leverage his considerable strength into a twist that broke the hog's neck.

It shuddered and laid still.

Wolfe's chest heaved as he tried to draw air into it. He fumbled with the rifle that had surprisingly stayed over his shoulder during the fight, pulled it around, and fired into the air. The drove ran off. He fired again, despite how precious every single round was, then fell to his knees and panted like a dog. Two dead animals, and he wouldn't let any of it go to waste.

CHAPTER NINE

B uddy was the first to see Wolfe dragging the massive carcass down the road. He barked and ran toward him. Jennifer followed. Billy Ray and Mary Lou watched from where they sat on an old section of guardrail.

"Mister Wolfe!" Jennifer cried as she clapped and skipped up to him. Buddy barked and nipped at the carcasses.

"Your dog will have to wait. Get the fire going. We have some work to do if we are going to preserve all this meat."

Jennifer clapped again and called to Buddy, but he was taken by the bloody carcasses, one inside the other. He started to bite at bloody skin, and the young girl had to wrestle him free. Wolfe kicked at the dog to drive him away, earning a glare from his adopted daughter.

"I was only trying to shoo him away," Wolfe meekly offered. She dragged the dog away, which was surprising since Buddy was stronger than the girl.

Wolfe continued dragging the big boar with the mid-size pig shoved inside the body cavity to make it easier to move them. When he arrived at the camp, he was glad of it.

"You know how to butcher a hog?" Wolfe asked.

"That I do, Mister Jim," Billy Ray replied, eyes sparkling with new life. "And Mary Lou is not bad with a blade and cutting board, either."

Wolfe flipped his knife around, offering it handle-first. Jennifer did the same with her pocketknife.

"Get us some thin pieces to cook now, and then we can start smoking the rest. It could take a while, but I like the thought of having enough to eat for more than just today."

Billy Ray and Mary Lou set to work with the most energy they had displayed since Wolfe met them. They nodded vigorously in agreement. Food was a powerful motivator, and they finally had more than they could eat.

Wolfe ate enough to satisfy himself before lying down to sleep. Someone would have to tend the fire, staying up through the night to smoke the hundreds of pounds of meat. Wolfe volunteered for the late shift. The others turned to the butchering and building an ad hoc smoker.

Wolfe did not know how they were going to carry all the meat, but he knew they would. It had been a good day, even though they had only covered ten miles. They were closer to Bradenton than when they started the day, and now they did not have to worry where their next meal would come from.

With food came strength, and with the drove of hogs, there was hope that the world was not entirely lost.

CHAPTER TEN

I t was almost a week before they were ready to go, but Billy Ray and Mary Lou had probably each gained five pounds. Their skin looked healthy, and their eyes were bright. Wolfe wondered how many people had suffered being malnourished in the aftermath of the war. It would have torn his heart out to see. What he saw two years later grated on his soul. Survival of the fittest.

It was hard on those who were not the fittest but were still trying to survive. Like the people of Ashland. Wolfe smiled to himself, thinking about them. He said a quick prayer that FEDCOM never tried to move back in, but if they did, the people would fight back. In his mind, that was what was needed more than the tyrants who filled Federal Command's ranks—decent people making a go at life without being preyed upon.

Just like Billy Ray and Mary Lou.

With the boar's hide hardened by the smoke and wood runners, they had built a sled on which the remaining meat could be towed. Wolfe wrapped the scavenged rope lead around his chest so he could haul the load. As long as they stayed on good road, he would be able to keep up the pace, still walking faster than the couple who was returning to health.

"Is he getting fat?" Wolfe asked.

Jennifer's eyes shot wide at the implication. "Not my Buddy!"

Wolfe was not so sure. The big dog was perfectly happy, eating his fill and sleeping until he was hungry again. Being on the road was good for him. Wolfe did not argue with Jennifer, but she glanced at the dog repeatedly, trying to gauge his new proportions.

"Maybe," she conceded.

They walked without talking since the wood scraping across the road surface made too much noise. They covered fifteen miles that day. According to a sign still standing by the side of the road, they had made it more than halfway to Little Rock.

"What do you think we will see when we get to the city?"

"How big is a big city?" Jennifer asked. She had led a sheltered life.

"Probably bigger than any place you have ever been before. It is bigger than Canon City, where they tried to put us in the fields to work. Before the bombs, Little Rock was about twenty or thirty times as large, I think."

"Where they wanted to eat Buddy." Jennifer scowled before she scratched the big dog's ears. His tongue fell from his mouth as he smiled at the attention.

"And that," Wolfe replied.

"Somebody wanted to eat your dog? I do not think I have ever been that hungry." Mary Lou made the statement to calm the young girl. Wolfe had his welding goggles to cover his eyes as he turned to the woman, but hers said she was lying. She *had* been that hungry.

Wolfe did not want to dwell on it. "What do you know about Little Rock?"

"I expect it is a mite different now," Billy Ray replied. "It was always the big city, but with good ol' country music playing in every store. Too many people for our taste, but good Southern hospitality, for what that is worth."

"No reason to think any different now. We give them the benefit of the doubt until they prove otherwise."

"You are a good man, Mister Wolfe," Mary Lou stated.

"He is the best!" Jennifer agreed, continuing to ruffle the dog's fur. "Maybe he *is* a little fat…"

"Wolfe?" Billy Ray wondered.

"Buddy." Jennifer laughed. She ran ahead, and the dog chased her. Wolfe pulled harder, not wanting her to get too far away.

The others hurried after him. Buddy stopped and his hackles went up as he faced the brush on the side of the road. Wolfe dropped the rope and started to run.

CHAPTER ELEVEN

A shotgun barrel poked out from behind a tree, wavering between the young girl and the dog. Jennifer held Buddy back, but she looked ready to let him go.

"Put it down or die," Wolfe called before he had his rifle ready. A heavy-set man stepped through the bush and onto the road. He kept his shotgun barrel up as he maneuvered to put Jennifer between him and Wolfe.

"You can call me Jim," Wolfe said casually, keeping his barrel up. "No need for anyone to die today."

"Well, Jim. I don't know you from Adam. You bring this group and an angry wolf and expect me to stand idle?"

"We are on our way to Little Rock, and last I saw, this is a public road."

"Not anymore."

"Then you need to talk to your maintenance crew because they are sleeping on the job." Wolfe sidestepped to clear his aim.

"Fair enough," the man replied, relaxing and moving the shotgun to the crook of his arm. "Name's Walton. Not one of *those* Waltons, even though this is Arkansas."

Wolfe hesitated. The man smiled.

"In this day and age, a man has to protect himself. Shoot first, ask questions later. It is a dangerous time to be alive." He cracked his shotgun to show it was empty.

Wolfe shouldered his weapon. "One should not play dangerous games during dangerous times," he cautioned. "My rifle is not empty."

The sound of wood scraping on pavement announced Billy Ray's and Mary Lou's arrival. They each had a hand wrapped in the rope as they struggled to drag the sled.

"Whatcha got there?" Walton asked.

"We don't share with no poacher!" Billy Ray shouted.

They all turned to look at him. Wolfe studied him to see if he was okay.

"If that is food, I am good. I have some livestock. If I had any shotgun shells, I would have as many rabbits as I could shoot. They play hell with my garden."

"Maybe we can do something about that. Do you have any thin wire to use as a snare?"

"I reckon."

"It is all in the knot," Wolfe explained. "Once through and caught, the snare has to cinch tight and stay."

The man shrugged. "I could use a little help, but I can pay with vegetables to go with your meat. Is that smoked?"

"Pork," Wolfe answered.

"That herd has been running through here, but it is led by a monster. Nothing I could do about them."

"You do not have to worry about that anymore." Wolfe tapped his rifle.

"I did not find any bullet holes. That carcass was clean, but it did have a broken neck," Billy Ray offered.

Wolfe hid his expression behind his welding goggles.

"How does a man break the neck of a beast like that?" Walton asked.

No one answered. Jennifer finally turned Buddy loose. The dog raced ahead, jaws wide, and ripped the shotgun out of Walton's hands. The man almost fell in his rush to get away from the German Shepherd mix and backed away, hands raised in surrender.

"Buddy!" Jennifer picked up the shotgun and handed it to him. She looked at the big man. "He does not like guns pointed at him, and neither do I."

Wolfe smiled at the brief tongue-lashing.

"I am sorry. You are decent people. It is not common nowadays."

"Maybe you can explain that to us over dinner," Wolfe suggested.

CHAPTER TWELVE

W alton lived in a two-story farmhouse. When they went inside, the upstairs was closed off. He found it easier to heat with the woodstove. A dozen head of cattle wandered around the pasture out back. A garden along the side of the house had expanded multiple times and spread toward the river across an overgrown field to the north.

Walton had plenty of telephone wire, although such things served no purpose any longer. Wolfe pulled the wire from the wall, yanking and tugging until he had a good twenty feet.

Walton took them outside to pick a few vegetables and look at where to set up snares.

While they worked, he talked. "I cannot send the cattle into that field because they get too close to the water. Gators will drag down a full-grown heifer."

"Alligators. When Arkansas becomes Florida, what has Florida become?" Wolfe asked more to himself than the others.

"That is a good question," Walton replied. "I think it is probably gone. Why else would the gators come up here?"

Jennifer tried to quiet the man, but he did not understand.

Wolfe frowned as he explained.

"I am sorry, Mister. I meant nothing by it. Hell, what do I know?"

"You know enough to keep this farm alive through it all: through the war, the refugees, scavengers, looters, and FEDCOM."

"FEDCOM?" Walton asked with a small shake of his head.

"You have never had Federal Command soldiers through here?"

"No soldiers. Nobody like that. Federal Command? Are they the government or something?"

"Or something," Wolfe agreed. "They were the only ones left with guns and military hardware, so they took over. Maybe they are western only, bordering on the Red Zone that cuts through the heart of the country."

"Red Zone? You say a lot of funny things, Mister."

"Radioactive. You are a blessed man, having no idea what that stuff is. Did you know there was a war?"

"Contrails in the sky. I figured something bad since everything was gone. Power mostly. Phones. Nothing worked, and then the people started streaming past."

Wolfe's ears perked up. "Which way, and what were they running from?"

"North at first, then south."

Wolfe waited for the man to explain further.

"With the power out in Little Rock, they were running up the Arkansas to the next big town. After a few weeks, they started coming back, heading south. They were an unhappy lot on the second trip. Not sure if they were the same people. They did not look like anyone I wanted to talk to."

"How come they never bothered you?" Wolfe asked.

Walton nodded toward the house where his shotgun was

now hanging over the fireplace. "They did. We scrapped. They ran."

Wolfe watched the man's eyes. Sad eyes. A proud man who had done things he never thought he would have to do. *Not all of them ran*, Wolfe thought.

"Looks to me like there is a Mrs. Walton." Wolfe redirected.

"Was. She died the second year after the fall. Something we took for granted until there were no more docs. The flu."

Wolfe toed a clump of dirt with his boot until it broke apart. Dredging up bad memories seemed to be on the day's menu. He had not intended to kick Walton while he was down. It had happened, nonetheless. "We shall dine well tonight, and tomorrow, we will go to Little Rock," Wolfe stated.

"I would like to come with you, but I have the cattle to take care of. They need something every day. I cannot leave them alone."

"Why would you want to come?" Billy Ray asked. "You have it pretty nice here. If we had this, we would not be looking to go anywhere else."

"What do you know about cattle?"

"My papa had a hundred head," Mary Lou replied.

"Trade you," Walton said without hesitation.

Wolfe could only watch.

"Why would you want to come?" Billy Ray repeated his question from earlier.

"Too many memories." Walton wiped his eyes and returned to the farmhouse.

Wolfe knew what he and Jennifer were doing. He had no idea about anyone else.

CHAPTER THIRTEEN

Come morning, Walton shook hands with Billy Ray and Mary Lou and nodded to Wolfe that he was ready to go.

"Simple as that," Wolfe said.

"What else is there?" Walton hefted a pack onto his shoulders that was heavier than he should have been carrying, but Wolfe was not going to counsel him. The man was an adult and would figure it out soon enough. In this world, one did not need a bunch of personal possessions. Survival gear was all that mattered. For Wolfe, it was food, ammunition, and water. For Jennifer, it was a couple of changes of clothes and their cookware. Wolfe pushed a two-wheeled cart with smoked beef and pork, raw vegetables, and even a bag of rough-ground flour.

It reminded Wolfe of the cart filled with supplies he had liberated from the wilders back in the Red Zone of Idaho. Maybe it was Utah. The longer ago it was, the less he remembered the particulars. He focused on what was important—the here and now.

"Miss Jennifer?" he asked.

The young girl skipped to him and took his hand as Buddy made one last run at the cow pen to bark at the stock. Jennifer called him back, and they pushed off.

"Fifteen miles to get to the southern end of Lake Maumelle, and that puts us less than ten miles from the heart of Little Rock."

Wolfe gave a curt nod and started walking. Jennifer caught up and stretched her strides to match his. Walton was a big man who looked not to have suffered the lack of food that nearly all other survivors had endured. Farmers with an eye toward defending what was theirs.

They were the wealthy ones in the new world.

Walton kept pace easily, his natural strides those of a hardworking man. Since he had ammunition and at Wolfe's urging, he had left the shotgun behind. It would draw needless attention. Without being able to fire back, it was more risk than it was worth. Wolfe did not expect to run across a stash of 12-gauge ammunition. Their one AR-15 would have to suffice.

Wolfe's bow was of limited use. He had two arrows he could rely on and only a few more that were solid. He knew how to make more but did not want to invest the time. Although he preferred the bow for certain targets, he knew that he would rely on the rifle because of the amount of ammunition he carried.

But he would not give up the bow. The day the ammunition ran out would be the day the bow would be worth more gold than anyone could carry.

Not that gold had a value anymore. Food. Clean water. Ammunition.

Wolfe looked at Walton. There was something more valuable than having those things. Someone with the knowledge to provide.

"We need more farmers." Wolfe spoke his thoughts out loud.

"You got that right." Walton turned back to look at his farmhouse one last time. Billy Ray and Mary Lou waved from the porch. He waved back before turning his attention to the road ahead. "What makes you say that?"

"Everything we have seen since we started the long road back home." Wolfe shifted his grip on the cart's handle. It rolled easily and was much better than their wood-runner sled. "Being able to provide for yourself with some to share makes you the heart of a new community."

"Like in the pioneer times. Back then, all people wanted was land to call their own. Maybe getting back to that will make us better people."

"We only want to get home to my wife and son." The welding goggles shielded Wolfe's eyes from the dawn's rays. The sun had barely climbed over the horizon. The early chill was invigorating, but they expected it to get hot later. If it did, they would stop and relax. If not, they would continue. The late summer had not yet given way to fall. Twenty-five miles would be eight hours of walking at their current pace. Wolfe looked proudly upon Jennifer. She would keep up, as she always had.

"I do not know what I want," Walton admitted.

"Strange for a man to take a journey without knowing where he wants to go." Wolfe glanced at the big man.

"Is it?" Walton replied.

CHAPTER FOURTEEN

By ten in the morning, Wolfe, Jennifer, Buddy, and Walton had reached Lake Maumelle. They stopped on a causeway that crossed the far western edge of the big lake. A light breeze created small, sparkling waves. The heavily forested southern side hid the shoreline from view. They stopped to enjoy the serenity of it all.

"A boat," Jennifer said. Wolfe turned his head to find a clear area of his goggles to peer through. He could barely make out the vessel in the distance.

Walton shielded his eyes with one hand while he squinted in the direction Jennifer was pointing. "Eyes are not as good as they used to be," he said before giving up.

Jennifer stared. "Two people, fishing."

"What do you say we go make some new friends?" Walton asked.

"Remember when you pulled your gun on us and almost got yourself shot?" Wolfe replied. "I am not in a hurry to go through that again anytime soon."

Walton clapped Wolfe on the back. "All's well that ends

well. We need information, right? We will learn what we need to know by asking questions."

"What do we need to know?"

Walton opened his mouth to reply and closed it when he had no answer.

"Maybe we can ask what the best way through Little Rock is?" Jennifer offered.

"There you are!" Walton smiled broadly and started walking.

"Why don't you take the cart for a bit? I think I am going to need my hands free. Just in case."

Walton's gaze flicked toward the rifle over Wolfe's shoulder before he nodded and stepped into place. He leaned into the handle to get the cart moving before settling into a good pace.

The road turned west at the end of the causeway, remaining a few hundred yards inland from the shore. Overgrown dirt roads led to cabins and campsites probably active before the war. They crossed an overflow from the lake and kept going. When they reached a marina, they saw their first people up close.

A family of four with three other adults were working on two different boats in the small harbor. A sign declared it to be Jolly Roger's Marina.

"Was he?" Walton mumbled as he struggled to get a clear look at the people.

"Was he what?" Jennifer asked.

"Jolly? Was Roger jolly?" He laughed heartily at his own joke. With the shackles of his farm life behind him, Walton had become a different person.

At the rolling laughter, a man on a boat looked up. He stared at the three standing on the bridge. Ahead lay an access road leading to the marina's parking lot.

"Shall we?" Walton asked.

The man on the boat gave no greeting, no sign that indicated how visitors would be treated. "I am not so sure they are the welcoming type. I say we move on."

"I'll go and talk to them. You can wait. If you hear me shout, take off. Save yourselves." Walton started pushing the cart. The turn was not far, and he made short work of it. He left the cart on the road and, with his head back, he whistled as he walked down the access road. Wolfe moved the cart to where it would not be visible by anyone who might casually look down the road. With his rifle in his arms and a round in the chamber, he settled in to wait. Jennifer and Buddy started exploring along the side of the road but ahead, where they would go in case of trouble.

Ten minutes later, Walton returned, still whistling.

"Good people, all!" he declared and waved for Wolfe to follow. He paused, waiting until Jennifer and the big dog returned. Together, they headed into the marina to introduce themselves and hopefully learn the best way through Little Rock.

CHAPTER FIFTEEN

"Jim Wolfe." The introductions were brief. The family stood in a line watching the newcomers. Walton remained true to his new form, all smiles as he walked from one to another, shaking their hands. "Sorry to intrude. We would appreciate any guidance you can give us to help us walk to the other side of Little Rock before we continue on our way."

A middle-aged man with a shock of dark hair strolled forward and offered his hand. Wolfe took it—calloused and rough. The hands of a man who was not afraid of hard work. Wolfe could respect that.

"Call me Danny Boyle," he said easily. "You will have to forgive us. We are not used to strangers, but our faith says all are welcome. We have been bad hosts. Can you forgive us?"

"Nothing to forgive," Wolfe replied, watching the group watch him. The children stared at his welding goggles. Children were hopelessly honest, and that prompted Wolfe to face them and kneel to be at their height. "My eyes were damaged in the war. These goggles help me to see."

"Stop staring," a woman who looked like a grown-up

version of the girls ordered. "I am sorry, Mister Wolfe. It is not in our nature to be rude, is it, girls?"

"No, ma'am," the children replied mechanically.

Her eyes remained sad while the corners of her mouth forced upward into the caricature of a smile. Her lips parted with the effort, revealing a missing tooth up front. Her smile quickly faded.

Danny stepped into Wolfe's line of sight. "What takes you beyond Little Rock?" the man asked.

"My wife and son. We are trying to get home to them. My daughter and I have been traveling for a while. We do not want any trouble, and we will not be staying long. I hope you don't mind."

"Why would we mind if a child of our Lord and Savior is trying to reunite his family!" Danny's voice took on a whole new tone and volume. A fanatical expression seized his features as he continued, "Our purpose is to support those in their righteous causes! Come with us, brothers and sisters. Tonight, we will worship in the house of the Lord and pray for his divine guidance to deliver our new friends into His hands. In the name of Christ our Lord. Amen!"

Danny Boyle thrust his fist into the air to highlight his final words. Wolfe mumbled "Amen" with the others. Jennifer stood frozen. Buddy found a bush nearby that needed to be marked and did what dogs do.

"I hope to be delivered into His hands," Wolfe said softly. "But not anytime soon."

"Amen to that, brother!" Danny Boyle declared.

"Get ready for church," the mother said and shooed the children away with pats on their behinds. She curtsied and followed the children toward the old harbor-office-turned-home. The other couple nodded to Wolfe and walked toward a fifth-wheel trailer set up in the marina's parking lot.

"We have smoked meat to trade if you need some," Wolfe said, trying to bring the man back to the present.

"We give freely of food, brother and expect you would do the same. Deny not a meal unto the hungry!" He moved next to Wolfe and tried to wrap his arm around his shoulders, but Wolfe dodged away.

"Sorry, Danny. I am not the hugging type," Wolfe said as he squared off against the man. Walton wrapped Danny in a bear hug and bounced him off the ground.

"Rejoice, brother!" Walton cried. "Of course, we have meat to share. That is what my good friend was saying. In trade for your assistance, everything is freely given, as you have shared with us."

Walton hugged him again and winked at Wolfe over the man's shoulder.

"As he said, freely shared." Wolfe decided discretion was the better part of valor and that ten pounds of smoked pork were a fair trade for two things: directions, and to disarm the fanatics. The sooner Wolfe could leave these people behind, the happier he would be.

Wolfe waved Jennifer away. She took the hint and grabbed Buddy to take him back to the road. Wolfe pulled out a wrapped slab of pork and handed it to Danny Boyle.

"Pork," the man said, studying it. "It was truly a blessed day when you stood on our path and shone your light on us."

Wolfe had no idea who he was talking about. Wolfe preferred the dark. Next time they approached a city, it would be at night, where Wolfe would be the one to choose whether they met with the locals or not. It would take someone special for him to reach out.

Then again, what would Lurleen think if he turned down God-fearing strangers, especially if he could provide what they so desperately needed? *If you were here, these decisions would be easy.*

But she wasn't, and Wolfe had to trust his gut. It told him to run as far and as fast away from these people as he could manage.

"We will be waiting on the road," he told Walton.

"We will walk with you, introduce you to the Pastor."

Wolfe had thought Danny Boyle was the pastor, but he missed the respect in the man's eyes as he said the words.

The Pastor.

Wolfe clenched his jaw. He had hoped he would not be going to war against another dictator. He hung his head and sighed. He would do what he had to do to get home to Lurleen and little JoJo.

CHAPTER SIXTEEN

W olfe pushed the cart toward the road, walking faster with each step. When he passed Jennifer, she looked back toward the marina.

"Are we not waiting for Mister Walton?"

"We are not, Miss Jennifer. He can catch up. We need to go as far and as fast as we can."

Jennifer ran after Wolfe, with Buddy close on her heels. The dog was indifferent to Wolfe's fears. His tongue lolled, and he bounced as he ran.

The creak and squeak of an old bicycle caught Wolfe's ears. He turned as Danny Boyle pedaled by on an old beach cruiser, coasted to a stop, and turned the bike sideways across the road. Wolfe slowed and stopped. He glanced behind him to see the rest of the group hurrying from the marina onto the main road. Walton waved. He did not look happy.

"You spooked me," Wolfe said. "It was never our intent to go into the city and meet people. Please forgive us. We have had some bad experiences during our trip."

"You are forgiven, but we will shield you, my brother, for

we wear the armor of the Lord." Danny Boyle's statements came straight from the pulpit, but Wolfe could not figure out which church. Danny's quotes were not from any bible Wolfe had read.

When the rest of the group caught up, they started walking again at a reasonable pace. The adults hurried the children along. No one complained. "You go this way much?" Wolfe asked.

"We attend the Sacred Survivors' Church every single day to pray for our salvation. It is a short five-mile walk that is good for the soul!"

A chorus of "amens" reinforced his claim. In words at least. Maybe not deeds.

"How many people attend this church?" Wolfe asked.

"The number of souls saved will equal the number of souls redeemed," the man replied, touching a finger to his nose.

Wolfe did not bother asking any more questions. Jennifer tried to talk to the smaller children, but their mother would not let them out of arm's reach.

Walton began a monologue on the wonders of farming that filled the void without allowing Danny Boyle the opportunity to climb back into his pulpit.

For that, Wolfe would be forever grateful.

After ninety minutes, Danny mounted his bike and rode ahead. Walton finally stopped talking. The woman they presumed was Danny's wife pointed to a sign up ahead. The Christian School of Little Rock.

"Is that where we are going?" Wolfe wondered.

"No," she replied. "That is where the people's disciples live. They always walk with us the rest of the way to the church."

"It looks like they have a church at the school."

"A small one, yes," the woman agreed. "The people need more room. The Sacred Survivors are many."

Wolfe looked ahead to see people streaming toward Little Rock.

"How many survivors are there?"

"Thousands!" She finally smiled a real smile. Wolfe shuddered and glanced at Jennifer without moving his head. She and Buddy were staying toward the side of the road away from their escorts.

"Did you hear that, Jim?" Walton interrupted. "Thousands!"

"Sounds like a lot of people," Wolfe muttered, shifting his eyes across their surroundings as they walked deeper into the suburbs and toward the main city of Little Rock. "Are they all as committed to the cause?"

CHAPTER SEVENTEEN

The old sign said Easter Seals. It looked like it had been a combination warehouse and office building. The faithful had turned it into the Sacred Survivors' Church. No one peddled Easter Seals anymore.

People streamed in from all directions. Wolfe continued to push the cart, quietly urging Jennifer to stay close. She wedged Buddy between them. The big dog's hackles were up and he panted, but not from the heat. He wanted the open air and the freedom to run.

They approached the door to find two men with clubs waiting. Wolfe raised an eyebrow toward Danny Boyle. Walton scowled.

"They are here to protect the faithful," Danny said with an innocent shrug.

"They look like bouncers. Since I can't take the cart or dog inside, we'll wait out here." Wolfe started walking at a right angle to the door.

Danny hopped on his bike and rode around to get in front of Wolfe. "This is getting old. Men do not get in other men's way. I assure you, there will not be a third time."

The man held his arms wide as he straddled the bike. "The time to rejoice is now. Take your place among the Sacred Survivors!" Danny nodded toward the doorway. Wolfe let go of the cart handle and sidestepped, ducking and coming back up with his arms wide and fingers ready to grab.

The men were coming, but slowly. They tapped their clubs on their palms. The faithful gave them a wide berth as they continued to stream into the building. They kept their eyes on the ground as they shuffled through the door. They had seen it before.

But they had not seen anyone like Jim Wolfe. He thought about using his AR-15, but he did not need it. It was only two men with clubs. They did not stand a chance.

They separated and raised their clubs to deliver heavy blows, but Wolfe was ready. He dodged forward, seized the men by their faces, and slammed their heads together before they could bring their clubs down. Their heads sounded like ripe melons hitting the pavement before they toppled. Dead or unconscious, Wolfe did not know.

Neither did he care. They should not have attacked him.

Danny Boyle's pastoral smile disappeared.

"You should not have done that, Mister Jim Wolfe."

Wolfe pulled his rifle from his shoulder and aimed at Boyle's chest. "We thank you for your hospitality, but it is time for us to go. We will be leaving now."

Jennifer restrained Buddy, who growled and lunged at the man on the bike. "That's right, Buddy," she said in a soothing voice. "He will be dog food if he tries to follow us."

A voice came from the doorway, and the faithful stopped and took a knee. Boyle dropped his bike and joined the others in kneeling. Wolfe's hair stood on end. He backed away from the cart until he could see both Boyle and the newcomer.

"Brother! I am Abraham. Please, pray with me."

Wolfe looked from the cowed followers to the man wearing a flowing purple robe. Wolfe was not impressed. "I think I will hold off on that right now. I just want to leave. I am not here to make trouble."

"I know, brother. Trouble has followed you here and caught you in its ugly tornado. We offer you peace, love's embrace, and a place where you can be yourself."

Wolfe smiled. "Perfect. I can be myself on the road out of here. Thank you, and take care."

"Maybe we should listen to him," Walton said softly.

"What for?" Wolfe had no intention of sticking around one minute longer than he had to.

"Abraham!" A woman's shrill call cut through the tension. "Come quick. A child…"

"Come," Abraham said without any sense of urgency. He waved for Wolfe and the others to follow and turned away without looking back. He walked through the doors and into the church. None of those kneeling stood.

Walton shook one of the faithful by the shoulder. "He's gone now. You can get up."

"We can rise only with Abraham's blessing." The young woman had no intention of standing until allowed to.

Walton kneeled next to her. "Why do you give him this power over you?"

"Why? Because we were starving, fighting, and dying. Abraham stopped all that. He only wants what is best for us. He is a peaceful and righteous man. We follow him because we want to, and we are better for it."

Walton stood to look at Wolfe. A movement caught Wolfe's eye. Abraham had stepped through the doorway with a baby in his arms. He bounced the giggling infant as a young mother followed, smiling widely, showing a neat row of bright white teeth.

"Where were we? Oh, yes, an impasse. Bring your cart in the side door, as well as your dog. All are welcome. We are friends to all." He turned the kneeling faithful. "Rise, my children! Go in and make yourselves comfortable. We have a special celebration today."

Abraham stopped two men in line and whispered to them. They bowed their heads and hurried to help the two bouncers. They hooked them under their arms and dragged them into the church.

"Come with me, please." Abraham gestured for Wolfe to follow. Walton took the cart in case Wolfe needed to protect them again. Jennifer and Buddy stayed close, but the big dog wagged his tail and bobbed his head at the man. He bent down, still cradling the baby, with the woman at his side. Buddy ran to him and fanned the air with his tail while getting his ears scratched.

Wolfe wanted to dislike the man, but Buddy was a good judge of character.

Abraham straightened and continued around the side of the building, where double doors led inside. These were not guarded or locked. He opened the door and finally handed the baby to the woman. She smiled when she took the infant. Wolfe pushed the cart through, with Jennifer grabbing Buddy as she passed and Walton holding the door for Abraham.

Once they were inside, they let the door swing shut. They were immediately thrust into the darkness. Wolfe pulled his goggles up and saw that Abraham and the woman walked slowly, hands out in front of them as they sought the door on the wall opposite the entry. No subterfuge. No games. Abraham found the handle and pulled. Wolfe yanked his goggles into place as the door opened and light from the inside the sanctuary streamed through.

"Come join us," Abraham called softly.

CHAPTER EIGHTEEN

W olfe waited for the applause to die down before pushing the cart to the doorway into the main hall and leaving it there. He leaned against the door frame with his arms crossed and studied the man on the stage.

Buddy liked him, and it jumbled his thoughts. He thought the man a despot, just like all the rest who hold power over others. The congregation appeared joyous in their praise, but he had seen the looks on their faces as they trundled toward the church.

Every day, they performed the same routine. For Danny Boyle and his clan, it was a five-mile one-way hike, and they made it without question.

No one should have that sort of power. But Buddy liked him. And now that Abraham was on the stage, the smiles appeared genuine.

"What do you think?" Wolfe whispered to Walton.

"A patriarch who the people worship. There were two thugs out front, but maybe that was to protect the faithful, not keep them in line. It is a strange day, Jim, and I do not have any answers."

"We have only given," Jennifer said.

Wolfe thought about it. Takers, like the wilders. He was not sure he needed any more takers in his life.

"We have visitors from afar!" Abraham spoke loud enough for all to hear. He was pointing at the doorway, where Wolfe and Jennifer could be seen. "Welcome them and make them feel like members of our family."

Abraham waved for them to join him. Wolfe slowly shook his head. Abraham took a knee and clicked his tongue. Buddy rushed through the door and jumped onstage. Jennifer ran after him slowly as the faithful clapped and cheered.

"If I were you, I would want to kill this guy," Walton whispered into Wolfe's ear.

"I am not his greatest fan," Wolfe conceded before waving to the crowd. He left his place in the doorway and walked to the stage. Walton went along out of curiosity.

Wolfe faced the crowd, holding out his hands for them to stop cheering. Abraham wrapped an arm over Wolfe's pack around the bow and slung rifle. "Jim Wolfe, Jennifer, and Walton!" Abraham raised his hands above his head and started clapping. The congregation joined him.

Danny Boyle must have told him our names.

Wolfe glanced over the crowd to find the man but could not locate him. There were too many people. It was like Canon City's dining room. Even had the same feel, except here, they were not lining Buddy up for the cooking pot. At least, he did not think they were.

Abraham gestured for the three to take seats by the door where Wolfe had left the cart. He shooed the big dog away after one last ear scratch.

Wolfe refused to sit, preferring to stand in the doorway. Walton and Jennifer sat, while Buddy lay at their feet.

The wheels in Wolfe's mind were turning. He wanted to learn more about this Abraham, the man who had brought peace to Little Rock after the end of the world.

False god, prophet, or just a man who could say what people needed to hear?

CHAPTER NINETEEN

After the hour-long service, the young mother, still carrying her baby, approached Wolfe, Jennifer, and Walton.

"Abraham has asked me to personally welcome you to the Sacred Survivors. If you would be willing to stay for a few days, we have accommodations set up for you. Are you two a couple?" she asked, pointing first to Jim and then to Walton.

The big farmer laughed so hard he could not speak. "Whatever would make you think that, little lady?"

"We do not judge," she said, holding one hand out to calm any offense.

"My daughter and I are traveling through to get back to my wife and son," Wolfe replied evenly.

"I see. Then we will provide two rooms if you are willing to share your time with us for a day or more. You may find that we have what you seek."

"As long as Lurleen is in Florida, you do *not* have what I seek." Wolfe's tone turned cold. Jennifer took his hand and squeezed it. Buddy sniffed but was not impressed by the woman. Only Abraham held sway over the dog. Walton offered to hold the baby since she kept trying to talk with her hands. She shifted the baby but held onto the little bundle.

"You are more than welcome to recharge your batteries before you continue your journey. Do not think unkindly of us, Mister Wolfe."

"You have electricity?"

"A simple expression. Maybe I should stop using it since it does not apply in the world of the Survivors, does it?"

Wolfe held her gaze but did not answer.

"Why do you wear those glasses?"

"My eyes were damaged in the war." Wolfe did not care to explain further.

"But you survived, and now *you* are one of the Sacred Survivors. You are truly blessed, Mister Wolfe, you and all your party." She shuffled her feet and looked over her shoulder toward the thinning crowd. "I will meet you out front and show you the way to the school where your rooms are waiting."

Wolfe chewed on the inside of his lip as he pondered the rest of their day. Jennifer continued to squeeze his hand. Walton dragged the cart backward and headed outside.

"What do you think we should do, Miss Jennifer?"

"I think I am tired. I would like to sleep in a bed, but if you think we should continue, I will go with you and not hold you back."

"I know you will. What do you say we take that room and see what tomorrow brings? I have questions, and the only place to get the answers is right here. I would like to stay long enough to peek behind the curtain."

Jennifer looked around. "I do not see any curtains, Mister Wolfe."

"Then we will have to find them first before we can see what is behind them."

Outside, Walton waited. "Staying or going?"

"Staying," Wolfe replied. "For tonight, at least."

"Sounds good. I am not opposed to hard work, but I have walked about as far as I want to walk today." Walton thought for a moment before continuing, "If you will have me, that is. I have no place to be and nothing to do. I was hoping I could tag along and see a bit of the world. I will take my turn with the cart. I am bigger than you, but not one-tenth as strong. Still, I will try to carry my own weight."

"You sound like Miss Jennifer," Wolfe said, smiling at the young girl. "I cannot turn a friend away. What would Lurleen think of me then?"

"Tell me while we walk." Walton nodded toward the young woman with the baby, who waved at them. "Looks like our escort is here. Do you know where she is taking us?"

"Someplace we probably do not want to be," Wolfe mumbled.

CHAPTER TWENTY

Wolfe was not surprised when they arrived at the Christian School of Little Rock. Danny Boyle and his clan passed while Wolfe was taking stock of his surroundings.

"You think that is the last we will see of them?" Walton asked.

"Only if we leave before tomorrow's services," Wolfe replied.

"They make that walk every day. So much walking to get nowhere."

"I believe the opposite," their escort interrupted. "They walk to receive their blessing. They are happy to do it because of where they live. The lake provides nourishment for the body, and the church provides nourishment for the soul. It is the best of all worlds."

She bounced the baby as she smiled.

"What is your name, Miss?" Walton asked.

"You can call me Katherine."

"Is that because it is your name?" Jennifer asked. Wolfe had to bite his lip at the innocent question.

"It is the name I have now, yes."

Jennifer nodded at the answer before running off with Buddy.

"Miss Katherine, we appreciate your kindness, but we would like a place to cook our dinner and to be left on our own, no disrespect intended. We have been on our own for a while, and we are not used to people."

"I understand. There is no need for you to cook your own dinner. We eat together. If you would care to donate some of your pork to the group, we will prepare it for all to enjoy."

Wolfe's eye started to twitch. *More taking.*

"We have a long journey ahead, and this will help us get there. Would you deny us our repast? We have already shared much with Danny Boyle and his family. Soon, we will be left with nothing. Is that what you intend?" Walton asked, putting the burden back on the young woman.

"Of course not. You are more than welcome to cook your own dinner, or you are welcome to eat with us. You are free to do as you wish." The tone of her voice suggested she was not happy with Walton's diplomatic refusal. She hurried toward a low building and went inside.

Wolfe stopped. The cart would not fit through the door.

"Wait, Miss Katherine," Walton called, through the opening.

She returned, looking less than patient. "What is it now?"

"We prefer not to leave our stuff out here," Walton said softly.

"No one is going to take your stuff. Bring it inside if you want, but there are no locks on the doors either." She put her free hand on her hip as if she had just played the trump card.

"Trust is earned when you have risked something for someone else," Wolfe started. "The way I see it, one hundred percent of the risk is ours. Danny Boyle took ten pounds of meat to bring us here. You want some of our food, too. You want us to take all the risks. What have you risked to earn our trust?" Wolfe kept his hands away from his weapons, but they remained within reach. He was not worried about Katherine but expected she could summon a small army of the faithful with one scream.

"We have brought strangers into our midst. Is that not enough?"

"No," Wolfe replied. "Come on, Miss Jennifer, we will be leaving now."

"Of course, Mister Wolfe." She dipped her head toward the woman with the baby. "Thank you, Miss Katherine. Come on, Buddy. Time to go hunt rabbits."

Jennifer skipped away. Wolfe nodded and turned the cart toward the main road, where they found Abraham slowly walking toward them with a small group of people in tow.

"I cannot believe what I am seeing." Abraham smiled broadly and spread his arms wide. His acolytes lined out to either side of him. Wolfe saw it as a showdown. Buddy treated it as a game, darting toward the line and away, barking at Abraham and the others as he pranced.

"We have overstayed our more-than-generous welcome. It is time for us to leave."

"Please stay, I insist." He smiled but only with his mouth, not his eyes.

"I do not feel safe here, Abraham," Wolfe parried.

"I cannot imagine why not, Jim. Have we not been welcoming enough? Katherine!" The woman cowered before reluctantly walking to Abraham. He took the baby from her arms, and one of the others led her away.

No words were spoken through any of it.

Abraham waved a hand and the line of men parted. "You can go."

"I would like to think I do not need your permission. I thought we were all free here." Wolfe did not know why he had to make that last dig, but he was spoiling for a fight. He had realized he had a great dislike for tyrants, those who held another's life in their hands to do with as they wished.

Even snuff it out at a whim.

"You are free to go. Please excuse my poor choice of words." Abraham crossed his arms and scowled.

"What is going to happen to Miss Katherine?"

"Nothing if you stay," Abraham countered.

"You see," Wolfe shook his head and moved his hand to the butt of his rifle, "that does not work for me. Using a human being as a pawn in your game makes you no better than those who destroyed this country."

"It is none of your concern. It is our business. We are not going to fight you, Mister Wolfe. I expect you do not start fights, but you end them. There shall be none for you to end. Please leave us in peace."

Wolfe stepped aside as Walton started pushing the cart. He smiled and nodded. "Nice meeting you boys. Y'all be cool now." He started to whistle on his way toward the road.

"Take your first right past the church. Hinson will take you through the city. Be careful since there are still a few areas that might be a little rough," Abraham advised.

"Obliged," Wolfe told him as he walked through the line of bodies, turning backward to keep Abraham in front of him. Jennifer had a hard time pushing Buddy, but eventually she managed, and the big dog gave up on trying to return to the compound.

Wolfe moved his rifle to the front, making sure there was a round in the chamber before he left Abraham's sight. Together, the three people hurried back toward the Sacred Survivors' Church.

They took a right as advised and jogged for a mile before stopping when Jennifer started to stagger. She apologized profusely, but Wolfe would have none of it. They hid in the backyard of an abandoned house, making themselves at home with a good meal cooked over a fire built from the fallen boards of stairs to the porch.

Wolfe took the first watch. Jennifer and Walton fell fast asleep. Wolfe waited until it was pitch-black before removing his goggles to see unhindered.

He circled the house, stopping when he heard a noise from the direction they had come. Four men with clubs were walking slowly down the street.

CHAPTER TWENTY-ONE

W olfe scowled. He moved through the darkness like a shadow within shadows. When he was behind the men, he walked into the middle of the street. "Can I help you?"

They crouched as they scattered, looking in his general direction.

"I expect you are looking for me. Well, you found me. Now what?"

One, braver than the others, stood and walked toward Wolfe. With a soundless sidestep, he moved away from the direction the man was heading.

"You know why we are here," the man started, cocking his head to better hear the answer. He raised his club while he inched forward. When he was within arm's length, Wolfe seized the club and ripped it away from the man, turning it on its former owner. The club impacted his head and he went down.

Wolfe tossed the club on the pavement.

"Maybe you can tell me why you are here. And use small words. I am just a country boy at heart." Wolfe moved quickly to the side. Two of the man dropped their arms, letting their clubs hang loosely by their sides. The third man's eyes were wide open, the whites showing all around his pupils. Wolfe watched him the closest.

One of the other two spoke. "We are here to bring you back into the fold."

"Never was in the fold," Wolfe replied, cueing the men to where he stood. He moved to the scared man and punched him in the side of the head, knocking him out.

"Cleetus?" one of the final two asked after hearing the body hit the ground.

"I do not think Cleetus is going to answer," Wolfe taunted. "Here you are, in the darkness, fumbling around looking for me. Carrying clubs. I do not want to hurt any of you, but you leave me no choice. You can walk away, or you can die where you stand."

Wolfe hated threatening people. Why could they not leave him alone?

"What would it take for you to come with us?" the first man asked.

"I am not going to come with you."

"We have good people in the church. Good people who farm, fish, and hunt. Good people who are trying to rebuild a world destroyed by greed. How can you not want to be a part of that?"

"All I saw was takers. People who wanted what I have. You have nothing I need, nothing I want. You need to let me go before more of your people get hurt."

"As you wish. I will relay your words to Isaac."

"Abraham did not send you?"

"Isaac did. One of the church patriarchs, an elder."

Wolfe wondered if his distrust was misplaced. Maybe Isaac was working outside of Abraham's desires.

No. Abraham pulls the strings, and we are all marionettes in his play.

"You need to be going now. Drop those clubs and gather your boys. You have a little walking to do to get back home. We will not be here when you come back, so it would save you a lot of time if you forgot about us."

Both men dropped their clubs before shuffling forward to find their comrades. Wolfe stepped silently away, watching intently as they picked up one, and then the other, carefully lifting them into fireman's carries and slowly walking away.

Wolfe waited until they were out of sight before returning to the yard. "We need to get going," he told the sleeping bags.

Walton grumbled, trying to wake from a deep sleep.

Buddy and Jennifer were nowhere to be seen.

"JENNIFER!" Wolfe shouted. Silence replied.

CHAPTER TWENTY-TWO

W olfe studied the area, looking for signs. Footprints in the dirt, not his or Walton's. "Watch our stuff. I have to go get my daughter." Wolfe did not wait for a reply. The men with clubs had been a ploy to distract him. It angered Wolfe that it had worked.

He jogged into the street. They had not gone this way, or he would have seen them. He headed around the block, looking for a way they could have gone. Trails and broken fences suggested they could have gone anywhere. His search would go better if he waited for them. He thought he knew where they were going.

Wolfe turned around and retraced his steps to the main road. He took a right and ran as fast as he could toward the church. He passed the two men shuffling along. One stumbled and fell. The other froze. Wolfe left them behind.

He made short work of the run, finding himself at the church after only a few minutes. He crept into the bushes surrounding the old Easter Seals building and waited. He listened and watched.

After thirty minutes, the two men appeared, still carrying their unconscious comrades.

They passed, turning at the corner. Wolfe followed them. A flickering light in a building here or there said that candles were the source. No electricity.

No FEDCOM either. Wolfe clenched his jaw so tight his cheeks started to hurt. He tried to relax, but he could not.

They were running from one enemy to the next. He was starting to lose faith in mankind. Humanity was generally good. It was the despots, those who would influence the others. What kept the good people from being in charge?

Wolfe finally relaxed. Because they could not dictate to their fellow man like the selfishly charismatic. The politicians of the new world. Wolfe preferred to leave people alone and let them do as they needed to do for themselves and their families. He would help anyone in need. He would fight anyone who tried to control him, like those who had kidnapped Jennifer. Their lives would be measured in hours instead of years.

He thought about Miss Bessie. She led the group out of necessity, not because she wanted to be in charge. FEDCOM wanted to be in charge. Abraham wanted to be in charge.

That subtle point made the difference.

Abraham was going to pay, right after Isaac suffered for his part in sending thugs after Wolfe and his family.

Wolfe caught up with the two men carrying the unconscious. He tripped one and punched the other in the face. The man's nose exploded and he reeled from the blow, dropping his load. Wolfe pounded him twice more, and he stilled.

The remaining thug struggled to get out from under the man he had been carrying. Wolfe pulled him free, dragging him along the ground before kneeling in the middle of his back.

"Where is Isaac?" Wolfe growled.

"I do not know!" the man claimed. Wolfe punched him in the back of the head, driving his face into the pavement.

"Where were you going right now? Where?"

"Back to the school. We have rooms there."

"Who else lives there?"

"Everyone and no one."

Wolfe punched him again. The man groaned from the impact.

"Where did they take my daughter?"

The man clenched his lips and refused to speak.

"I am a firm believer in not torturing another human being, but I feel I have to take out my anguish on something, and the only one available is you. Nothing matters more to me than my family. If you had one, you would know. You were sent after me for the sole purpose of taking my daughter. You had your orders. Now I need you to tell me what they were to save yourself a great deal of pain."

The man tried shaking his head. Wolfe broke three of his fingers before he could finish. When he started to scream, Wolfe clamped his mouth shut.

"I asked you a question. I deserve an answer."

The man started to pant from the pain, but at least he stopped trying to scream.

"When I break your wrist, you will forget all about your fingers."

"Stop, please." He closed his eyes and rested his head on the pavement. "Isaac's compound."

"You will have to forgive me, but I do not know where that is. Please tell me more." Wolfe maintained the pressure on the man's back, keeping him from moving. He had a tight grip on his wrist in case the man reneged on his help.

"Take a right at the next block. Down on the right. You cannot miss it."

"When I let you up, you need to do the right thing and go home. Anything else will not help you live a long life."

"What about them?" the man asked.

"That is the right thing. I will set them aside. When they come to, they will find their way home, or the faithful will find them. In either case, there is nothing you can do for them right now. Go on. Get yourself home." Wolfe jumped up and backed away.

The man slowly got to his feet. He cradled his hand with the broken fingers as he staggered away.

Wolfe headed into the shadows. He skimmed past the man and hit the corner at a dead run. He accelerated down the side road, quickly pulling up. There was a barricade with men, smoking and watching. A razor-thin crescent moon provided little light. Although Wolfe could see as if it were daytime, the guards could probably detect movement. He would have to go around.

He turned into the brush and found himself up against a wall. It was not a barrier to him getting what he wanted. He leapt and pulled himself up. The other side was clear. Wolfe eased over, hung until he was steady, and dropped to the ground. He flexed when he hit.

Darkness and silence were his friends. He stayed in the shadows while he moved through the backyard of a massive house. There was a gate in the front. He hesitated. The sound of a squeaky hinge had no natural counterpart. He did not risk it, jumping to grab the top of the wall next to it.

Wolfe lay prone on the top stones, watching and listening.

There was a commotion not far away.

"Good doggy." Wolfe could barely make out the words, but they were enough. He let himself down and started to move in the direction of the voices.

"Buddy will bite you! You better back off," a young girl's voice replied.

Wolfe stopped behind a tree and leaned out to take a look. A group of four men surrounded Jennifer and the big dog, while four more men stood in front of the house. A piece of meat appeared in one of their hands. Buddy hungrily gulped it down while the man eased two ropes around the dog's neck. When Buddy finished, two men pulled in opposite directions.

Buddy did not take kindly to that and started jumping and snapping, but they had the leverage. The wolf-cross soon tired, panting heavily from the ropes' pressure on his throat. Jennifer struggled against the rough hands that held her, to no avail. She started to sob.

Wolfe broke from cover and started to run. The sound of a gunshot surprised him. Two more steps and he felt the pain. His leg was on fire. He turned ninety degrees and headed for cover.

"Get her inside!" The eight men out front scrambled to comply. Another shot buzzed past Wolfe's head. His leg felt more and more wooden as he sought cover. He found a tree and placed his back against it.

He flipped his rifle off safe and peeked out. Then he peeked from the other side. A man on the upper floor with an oversized scope. A night-vision scope. Wolfe popped out from the other side of the tree, bracing the rifle for a snap shot. It hit a sandbag piled at the front of the window, which made the sniper hesitate. Wolfe's second shot took him in the face. He disappeared from the window.

Wolfe took stock of his situation. His leg was on fire. Grazed, but deep enough to have dug through the muscle. He pressed his hand against it, unsure of what to use to bandage the surface wound.

Buddy continued to fight, growling between gasps.

And Wolfe needed help. He stepped into the open, aimed, and fired. One man holding a line went down. Buddy launched himself at the second man. It was over in seconds. Wolfe limp-loped to the big dog and pulled him from his prey. He ripped the ropes off and looked at the building, which was a mansion from an earlier time. A circular driveway. Outbuildings. But they had taken Jennifer inside the main building.

"Come on, Buddy. We have work to do."

CHAPTER TWENTY-THREE

Wolfe did not go straight at the house. He used the darkness to his advantage. He limped his way around the outside, keeping Buddy close to him. The dog started to whine.

"We'll get her. Soon."

The back door looked to be the only other way into the house. Wolfe squinted against the pale candlelight glowing inside. He caught a glimpse of Jennifer. They were taking her upstairs. She was fighting them all the way.

"Soon," Wolfe whispered. A trellis. A downspout. "Wait here."

He knew the decorative woodwork would not support his weight. He chose the downspout to get him close to a second-floor window. Before he started to climb, Wolfe rubbed a handful of dirt into the wound, and then another. He caked the mud until it stopped bleeding. Wolfe started to climb while the big dog pranced back and forth, upset at having to remain behind. "Stay."

Wolfe's leg did not want to cooperate, forcing him to hold on with his arms and good leg and pull himself up six agonizingly slow inches at a time. He pulled and adjusted, pulled and rearranged, pulled, and pulled some more. The second-story window he made it to was dark. He hugged the pipe and reached a free hand over to slide the window up. He dug his fingernails in and pushed.

It would not budge. *Going through,* he thought. Climbing to the roof was out of the question. He unslung his rifle while still hugging the pipe, and used the butt to break the window and clean the glass from the edges. The window breaking sounded like the loudest alarm, but it could not be helped.

Wolfe wrapped a leg over the sill and pulled himself through, finding an occupied bedroom. The young female sat up with her covers pulled tightly under her chin, eyes wide with fear. Wolfe walked through. She followed him with her eyes as he opened the door and peeked into the hallway. Two men stood by a door a few feet away. They carried clubs, which seemed to be the weapon of choice for the faithful. Wolfe charged.

The breaking glass had made them aware, but they were not ready for the fury of Wolfe's attack. He destroyed the closest man's face by delivering a fistful of knuckles, forcing the second to stumble backward because the first did not even slow Wolfe down. Wolfe caught the guard and slammed him face-first into the wall before twisting his head halfway off. He dropped the limp body and kicked the door in.

An immense bedroom greeted him. A woman in silk pajamas stared, but Wolfe did not care about her. The man in silk boxers held Jennifer from behind, a knife at her throat.

"Put your rifle down, Mister Wolfe. I think you understand what I'm capable of. Neither of us wants that, so put the rifle down and your hands up."

"You do not know what I am capable of. I take it you are the one who calls himself Isaac?" Wolfe moved to the side, toeing the ruined door shut.

Isaac pulled back on Jennifer's hair, making her yelp. Wolfe sidestepped across the room. The woman tried to move away from him, but he watched her closely until she was within arm's reach. He grabbed her and forced her in front of him. Wolfe balanced the barrel of his AR-15 over her shoulder.

"I think you overestimate Sheila's importance to me," the man said. The temperature in the room seemed to drop.

Wolfe pulled the trigger, sending a high-powered rifle round past the man's ear. The woman fell to the floor with her hands over her ears. Jennifer tried to fight Isaac, but his grip was too strong.

"I guess we are at an impasse," Isaac stated. He flinched when Wolfe fired the rifle, but he did not give ground.

The door slammed open, revealing two, then four men.

"Take him," Isaac ordered. The first men edged into the room but stopped when Wolfe turned his rifle on them. "Not willing to follow orders, gentlemen?"

The first man took a deep breath and scowled as he rushed forward. Wolfe pushed the silk-clad woman into him and stepped back. The man stumbled over her and Wolfe cold-cocked him with the butt of the rifle. The second man met the same fate. The last two tussled for a moment before Wolfe put both of them in their places.

Isaac had used the distraction to leave, taking Jennifer with him.

CHAPTER TWENTY-FOUR

W olfe ran through the door, face-first into two more men storming down the hallway. He seized each by an arm and threw them down the hall. They hit the ground and rolled, coming quickly back to their feet. Footsteps pounded down the stairway. Wolfe shot the closest man in the leg. The second did not get the message.

He crouched, growled, and charged. Wolfe shot him in the chest before turning and running after Isaac and Jennifer.

The front door was open. There were no sounds from inside. Wolfe ran outside and yelled for Buddy, and the wolf-German Shepherd mix came running. "Where's Jennifer?" Wolfe asked.

The big dog wagged his tail and sniffed around but didn't find anything. Wolfe turned around and limped back inside, Buddy headed around the steps and toward the kitchen. The dog started growling.

Wolfe slowed since his leg had gone from numb to hurting again. The pain made him wince with each step. He found Isaac holding Jennifer behind a center island. Sparkles appeared before Wolfe's eyes. He expected that was from losing blood, so his time to act was drawing down.

He brought his rifle up. "Duck," he said, and Jennifer jerked to the side. Isaac moved the knife back toward her throat. The AR-15 barked, filling the kitchen with the sound of the explosion driving the bullet down the barrel, across the short space of the kitchen, and into Isaac's breastbone. The man was thrown backward, bounced off the counter, and left a blood smear from the exit wound as he toppled.

Jennifer ran to Buddy and threw her arms around his neck. Only then did she see Wolfe's injury.

"We need to get out of here," Wolfe mumbled. Jennifer threw his arm over her shoulder as she unbolted the back door. They nearly tumbled down the stairs on their way out. Buddy ran alongside, watching and sniffing. The guard dog had failed his friend once, but would not do so a second time this night.

They staggered and limped down the road until Wolfe thought he was going to pass out, then headed for the bushes along the side of the road, finding a nook in which to secret themselves. Jennifer took Wolfe's rifle and stood guard while her adopted father passed out. She kept Buddy close as she shivered against the night and fear.

Jennifer jerked awake at the sound of voices nearby.

CHAPTER TWENTY-FIVE

Jennifer nudged Wolfe to get him to wake up, all the while kicking herself for falling asleep. Buddy was sound asleep too, laying half on Jennifer and half on Wolfe, keeping them both warm and protecting them from the early morning dew. The night had been too short, and morning had arrived too soon.

The young girl was torn. She decided that hiding was their only option. Mister Wolfe would not wake up, but his slow and even breathing said he was alive.

She could not see out. That meant that they could not see in. She listened to see if they were coming her way. Buddy's ears perked and twisted to hear better. He started to whimper and wanted to get up. She tried to hold him down, but he only got louder, finally barking his dismay.

A big hand pulled the bushes aside, and Abraham looked at them. Buddy stepped on Wolfe's leg in his rush to see his friend. Wolfe cried out and his eyes popped open. With the morning sun came pain. He fumbled with the goggles around his neck. Jennifer helped when she saw he was unable to make his fingers work properly.

"There you are. I hope you are okay," Abraham said softly, gesturing for Jennifer to come out of hiding. She shook her head. "We cannot help Jim if you stay in there."

She sighed heavily and crawled out from behind the bushes. Abraham waved at a man and woman nearby. They worked their way into the opening and carefully lifted Wolfe out. Abraham himself cradled Wolfe's leg as they carried him to Isaac's house.

"NO!" Jennifer cried. She tried to break free of the grip Abraham had with his other hand. She tore at his wrist with her fingernails, fighting to get free. "No!"

"I know what happened. Isaac was acting without my permission," he pleaded with the young girl. "You are safe with me."

"I am not so sure," Wolfe mumbled.

"I will try to prove myself to you. If we wanted to do anything untoward, you could do nothing about it. Please, Mister Wolfe, let me try to redeem myself and the flock in your eyes."

Buddy's tongue flopped out the side of his mouth as he ran along happily beside the group. Jennifer dragged her feet, pulling Abraham backward while he tried to keep up with the couple moving forward. Abraham finally let go so he could focus on not shaking Wolfe's leg.

Jennifer ran a few steps away before realizing that no one was going to chase her. Buddy was torn about who to follow. He started to whimper again.

Hanging her head in surrender, she stumbled along, falling behind as the four people hurried forward. They went into the house, leaving the door open. They turned to the right, heading into the living room. Jennifer did not remember anyone getting killed in that room.

Maybe it would be okay.

She walked in with Buddy by her side. The woman had

a basin of water and a rag and started washing Wolfe's wound while Abraham and the other man watched. A glass of water was close to Wolfe's head. A needle and thread were at hand, ready to stitch the wound closed once it was clean.

Buddy wedged his head against Abraham's side, earning an ear-scratch for his troubles. Jennifer moved closer, finally getting a good look at the injured man. He was pale and sweating and he looked gaunt, as though he had lost ten pounds overnight.

"Did Mister Wolfe do all the damage in here?" Abraham asked, watching Jennifer closely.

She nodded, not taking her eyes off her adopted father.

"Isaac has been punished for his actions, as you well know. I apologize that it happened. I had no idea what he was planning. I should have been more aware."

Jennifer glared at the man.

"I would be angry, too," he agreed. "Let me get you something to eat."

He gestured for her to follow, but she vigorously shook her head, eyes darting toward the kitchen.

"Oh, that! It has been cleaned up already, but I understand. You still do not want to go. I will get you something to eat. And for Mister Wolfe, too."

Abraham was gone for five minutes. When he returned, he had a plate of cut-up fruit, hard-boiled eggs, strips of white meat that looked like chicken, and the ultimate delight, a cinnamon sticky bun.

Jennifer was tentative at first but dug into everything. She tried to leave the bun, but could not resist. After her first bite, she ate until it was all gone. That was when Wolfe opened his eyes and rolled his head, trying to orient himself.

"You are in the living room of my former number two."

"Am I your prisoner?"

Abraham laughed. "Oh, heavens, no. You are free to go whenever you are able to walk."

"Now sounds good." Wolfe forced himself to sit up, suffering through a wave of nausea with closed eyes before trying to see again.

Wolfe stood on unsteady feet and took one step. His injured leg buckled. Abraham caught him and helped him back to the couch.

"Maybe not now, but soon."

"Whenever your body tells you it's ready, Mister Wolfe. I have to apologize for the activities of my number two." Abraham took a knee before the couch to look up at Wolfe.

"I have never seen a leader who did not know what his people were doing. You are too hands-on. Forgive me if I do not believe you."

"There is nothing to forgive, Mister Wolfe. I would not believe me, either." Abraham picked up the plate from where he had set it aside. "Please eat something, and here's water, too. You need it to get your strength back so you can be on your way."

Wolfe agreed with the man and ate everything that remained, despite his stomach's protests. He drank one glass of water. The woman who had cleansed the wound refilled it. Wolfe drank that and a third before he stopped. They laid him down on the couch and covered him with a blanket, and he fell sound asleep.

"What do we do now?" Jennifer asked.

"Where is Mister Walton?" Abraham asked.

CHAPTER TWENTY-SIX

J ennifer crossed her arms and stared at the floor.

"No matter. If he is hungry, there is room at our table for him. He seemed like a down-to-earth guy." Abraham studied the girl before tipping her chin up so she would look at him. "This is Evie and Pierre. They are here to nurse Mister Wolfe back to health. If you need anything at all, you have only to ask. The faithful need to be tended to, now more than ever. I need to redeem myself in their eyes, too. There was a great deal of gunfire here last night. They are not used to that. *I* am not used to that, and it is something we need to pray about as we return to our peaceful ways."

He glanced over his shoulder at the young girl, his eyes glistening as he frowned.

Jennifer sat on the floor and leaned against the couch.

"Your dad will be just fine," Pierre said. "He only needs rest. Do you play chess?"

"I do," Jennifer replied.

A board materialized in Evie's hands and she set it up on the coffee table. Soon they were embroiled in a game, then Jennifer started nodding off. They brought her a blanket and a pillow. She laid on the floor next to the couch. Buddy snuggled in next to her, and they both fell fast asleep.

They slept on and off for the rest of the day, not seeing anyone except Evie and Pierre. Anything they wanted—water, food, blankets—was quickly provided. They even acquired a new pair of jeans to replace the ones torn by the bullet and caked with blood.

The second morning after Isaac's departure from the world of the living, Wolfe was finally able to stand without assistance. He walked with a limp to avoid stretching the stitches.

Evie and Pierre said it was a miracle. Abraham arrived to check on Wolfe's progress and was stunned.

He considered it nothing less than divine intervention. Wolfe knew it was because of whatever had happened to him in that mine immediately after the bombs fell. Two years he had waited for the radiation to lessen, and when he came out, he was a different man.

Stronger, and his hair was mostly white, the last bits of brown clinging to the tips. His eyes shielded by the welding goggles to keep the sun from causing him extreme pain.

Maybe it was a miracle, but Wolfe did not feel special. He was a man trying to get home. People counted on him. Jennifer. The downtrodden in the communities through which he passed.

Just a man.

"Are you still going to leave us?" Abraham asked.

"Yes." Jim Wolfe did not mince words.

With Jennifer and Buddy by his side, they started toward the door. Outside, Walton waited with the cart.

"Did they get you, too?" Wolfe asked.

"No." The big man smiled. "I came in on my own. I had to find out what happened to you. Seems like you caused quite a ruckus."

Wolfe limped down the stairs, leaning heavily on the rail. His bandage started to turn red from the freshly leaking wound.

"Maybe you should rest up a bit longer," Walton advised. "There are no more men with clubs if you were wondering. That was something Abraham did away with as soon as he found out what Isaac had been doing."

"Which was?"

"Power, Mister Wolfe," Abraham said from the porch. "Isaac was using his position to dominate the faithful. Plus, he was using his position to exploit the vulnerable, and by that, I mean women."

Wolfe was not happy. He pulled Jennifer close to him. Buddy ran up and down the steps. Abraham produced an old tennis ball and threw it. The big dog was off like a shot.

"Jennifer is safe, as well as everyone else. I have a lot of work to do to re-earn the confidence of the Sacred Survivors."

"I thought you already had the power," Wolfe countered.

"I do, but I need to re-earn their trust and respect. I lost that, in my own mind, by having a man like Isaac so close." Buddy returned with the ball but would not give it back. He kept chewing while Abraham grabbed for it. Jennifer tried to tackle Buddy, but it didn't work. She ended up in the grass, and the ball got worked over until it was nothing but shredded rubber and felt. Buddy looked for the next ball Abraham would throw.

"I only had that one," he pleaded. Buddy did not understand. He settled for a knotted rag instead, thrown as far as Abraham could.

Walton left the cart to help support Wolfe.

"You probably should not go anywhere until you stop leaking." Walton could see his reflection in Wolfe's welding goggles.

"I think you might be right." Wolfe turned to Abraham. "I would like to ask for your hospitality for a few more days."

That was not easy for Wolfe. He was not convinced Abraham had known nothing of his number two's misuse of power. Staying a few more days would help clear up questions that Wolfe had about the faithful. Who would prevent it from happening again?

CHAPTER TWENTY-SEVEN

"Would you just climb in?" Walton held out his arm for Wolfe to grab. The cart was empty, its previous contents locked in a shed on the property of the former number two.

"I do not want to go."

"Take it like a man and get in." Walton looked impatient. Jennifer started to giggle. "They are going to give you some kind of award."

"I have not been to church in a while. What about lightning?" He thought back to his time with the settlers, when he thought he was with Lurleen but was not.

"You were in church a few days ago. In!"

Wolfe was torn between doing what he wanted and doing what others wanted. He reluctantly threw his injured leg over the edge before taking Walton's hand to get the rest of his body inside. Jennifer skipped along beside the cart as Walton grunted and pushed.

"You have been eating far too well," Walton grumbled.

Wolfe looked at himself. He had no extra bodyfat, being

on the lean side if anything. "Maybe you are out of shape," Wolfe parried before turning to look ahead. The former Easter Seals building was not far, maybe two blocks. They took their time getting there. The faithful streamed past, nodding respectfully before continuing.

"They have a whole new attitude, don't they?" Walton asked.

"Seems like it," Wolfe agreed. He watched them more closely. The tension he had seen before was gone. Even Danny Boyle smiled when he passed, but he hurried ahead, making his wife and children run to catch up. They nodded politely as they jogged by.

The faithful crowded the church, more than there were before. Maybe Isaac had driven some away or had his small army doing other jobs, not attending church like the rest.

Wolfe did not see how he would fit inside. He once again decided he did not want to go. "No room. Back to the house."

"No *bueno*," Walton replied with a chuckle. He helped a reluctant Wolfe out of the cart.

"We are going to have words about this," Wolfe promised.

"I look forward to them, my friend." Walton's smile was sincere and warm. It disarmed Wolfe and sent him limping inside.

"You do not have to tell me. I guess we are sitting up front?"

"Of course." This time, it was Jennifer who seemed to know things Wolfe did not.

Abraham worked his way through the faithful, shaking hands and sharing kind words. When he finally made it to the stage, he called for quiet. He started with a prayer and a call to grace, forgiveness for those who were lost, and glory for those who had been found.

Wolfe watched in silence, avoiding the obligatory amen.

Abraham said his final words and then asked Wolfe to come to the stage. Wolfe limped up the short steps and toward the center, where Abraham waited.

"I only have one question, Mister Wolfe. Why do you do what you do?"

"I am not one for speaking in public. I keep to myself usually." Wolfe spoke softly, but it was quiet in the room. Even so, some in the back strained to hear. Wolfe looked at Jennifer, who smiled back. The simplicity of it all struck him. Had it not been for the war and the tragic fallout afterward, they would have never met. Would her life have been better or worse? He had no idea. Wolfe only did the best he could. "I do not much care who started the war or why. That is ancient history. We are left to pick up the pieces. Whether we are sacred as survivors, I do not know nor care. What I do know is that if I want the world to be a better place, without another nuclear war, then I have to make sure men like Isaac are not allowed to prey on people like you. That men like Abraham are praying for you."

The congregation gave a hearty "Hear, hear!" Wolfe waited for the din to die down before continuing.

"I did not want to get involved here or anywhere else, but sometimes, we cannot stand by and let things happen. We cannot let bad things happen to good people. Our wives. Our daughters. Our brothers and our sisters. We have to fight against those who would take. In the Red Zone, they are called the wilders. They know no law but the survival of the fittest. I have found in my travels after the war that it is not much different in the Clear Area. Fight for yourselves, and fight for your families. If you do not, the Isaacs of this new world will crush you under their feet. If Abraham asks you to do something hard, you listen. If he asks you to do something against your conscience, you refuse."

Wolfe turned toward Abraham and held his gaze until the man nodded. Wolfe did not have any words left, so he waved and stepped off the stage. Abraham walked to the center and held up his arms to join the Sacred Survivors in clapping their appreciation. When they finished, he gestured for Wolfe to return to the stage.

"A token of our appreciation for your service to a grateful nation, a new nation that is better because of men like you. There is no medal or trophy because you have been clear that you wanted one thing—to get home to the rest of your family. We can offer you bicycles to hopefully make your journey a little bit easier." Abraham waved, and two of the faithful rolled modern-looking mountain bikes to the front. There were only two.

"But Walton..." Wolfe started.

"Always thinking of other people before yourself. You have a gift, Jim Wolfe. Never lose that. Walton has asked to stay, to be my number two. He has not been influenced by anyone here, least of all me. But, and this is important, he has been on the receiving end of the example you set. He brings that to us, a piece of you to stay here while you continue your journey."

Walton stood and cheered. Wolfe wondered why he had waited to spring it in front of a full church. But trying to influence others to do what they did not want to do? Wolfe would leave that to those who needed to be taken down.

Wolfe waved to the Sacred Survivors. Jennifer rushed to the stage and hugged him. He wrapped a protective arm around her. Buddy bounced onto the stage, wagging his tail furiously. He was happy to get an ear scratch from Abraham.

"Buddy knew," Jennifer said.

"Buddy let bad people sneak up on me too many times in the Red Zone for me to trust that dog."

Jennifer punched Wolfe in the stomach. "Buddy's a good dog!"

"Yes, Buddy's a good dog." Wolfe decided discretion was best since he would not win that battle. They had a long road ahead. He aimed to win the war.

CHAPTER TWENTY-EIGHT

Two days later, Wolfe and Jennifer sat astride their bikes. The most precious part of the gift was the tire repair kit and air pump. He wondered if they would be able to ride the whole way. He hoped

First the truck that helped them cover five hundred miles, then the bikes that would help them go fifty miles a day. The big dog could run alongside, or he could ride in the cart with the arms connected to the back of Wolfe's bike, even though it was stuffed with other supplies.

The faithful had been too generous to Wolfe and Jennifer. Walton had wanted to make sure they had enough food to make it without stopping. Wolfe figured they would find plenty to eat along the way. He had his rifle and bow, and Jennifer had her blowgun. Maybe they would stop south of Little Rock and scavenge the materials for another blow gun and maybe a few arrows.

Wolfe reached out and Walton took his hand, shaking firmly. Then Abraham. They gripped each other's hands for a while before letting go.

"I might have misjudged you," Wolfe admitted.

"Only God judges, but I am glad you gave me a chance."

"Only because of him." Wolfe nodded toward the big dog, who was getting the last of his ear scratches. "If he had not liked you, it would have been a different story."

"I am sure. Peace, brother."

"And to you." Wolfe turned to Jennifer. "Ready?"

She still looked uncomfortable, although they had been working with her for two days. She had never ridden a bike before.

"Once you get it, you will be an expert. Give it five minutes." He pushed off and started pedaling, but slowly.

Walton gave Jennifer a running start. She pedaled to keep up before realizing she had been turned loose. She tried to wave and almost lost control, so she returned her hands to the handlebars and focused on the road ahead. Buddy loped easily alongside. Wolfe worked the bike until he found the right gear and settled into an easy, distance-eating pace. He stayed even with Jennifer.

"Next stop, South Little Rock. Pretty soon we will turn east, and nothing will stop us until we hit Florida."

Jennifer shook her head and smiled. "There will be something, Mister Wolfe. I would bet my next meal on it."

The End
Nightwalker, Book 6

If you like this book, please leave a review. Your opinion matters to me. I will write books 7 & 8, but when? If we get enough reviews, it will be sooner rather than later. I have only so much time to craft new stories. Help me invest that time wisely. Plus, reviews buoy my spirits and stoke the fires of creativity.

Don't stop now! There's more...

ABOUT THE AUTHOR

Frank Roderus wrote his first story—it was a western—when he was five. It was really awful, as might be expected, but his mother kept that typed and spell-checked short story tucked away until the day she died.

Later, Frank became a newspaper reporter, thinking that books are written by authors which he most assuredly was not. He kept trying to write though, and eventually did it wrong enough to learn how to get it right. That first sale, a young adult novel published by Independence Press, was more than thirty years and a good many books ago.

As a journalist, the Colorado Press Association awarded Frank Roderus their highest award, the Sweepstakes Award, for the best news story of 1980, and the Western Writers of America has twice named Frank recipient of their prestigious Spur Award.

Frank passed away at age 73 in December 2015.

NOTES - CRAIG MARTELLE

WRITTEN SEPTEMBER 22, 2019

Thank you for reading this installment of the Nightwalker! You have my sincere appreciation for sticking with us and reading our stories.

I had finished this book a while ago, but it took a while to get it through our quality control process. It should be good to go, ready for prime time!

For this volume, it was time to put FEDCOM in the rearview mirror, literally, and get Jim and Jennifer on the road home. They covered a lot of ground before arriving in Little Rock. Sometimes there is no adventure on the road, especially when they can drive and eat up a lot of miles.

And then it takes them a week to go a mile. One never knows in the world of the Nightwalker.

I've been home for six weeks straight! Fall has arrived, and more so than just on the calendar. The leaves have all fallen and temperatures have dropped. Last night was the first temps below freezing which signal that the start of winter is not far behind. We're ready. I might need to get some more pellets for the stove, but with my truck, I can have them load a ton into the back and then drop them off right in my garage. Easy peasy.

Phyllis is slowing down as she approaches the end of her 12th year. She's still good, just pacing herself. I think she's growing hard of hearing as she only sometimes hears the UPS guy which then earns him a good barking. Otherwise, she'll sleep through the truck's arrival, door slamming, and knocking. Which is okay. She's earned a good sleep.

Short author notes. I almost forgot to write them, but almost isn't the same as completely forgetting. Back to the grind. Executioner 7 is over halfway finished and that one is shaping up to be a great exploration of the law and the crimes of the rich affecting the rest of the galaxy. An interesting legal challenge, to say the least.

That's all I have for now. Thank you for coming on this journey with us.

Peace, fellow humans

BOOKS BY CRAIG MARTELLE

Craig Martelle's other books (listed by series)

Terry Henry Walton Chronicles (co-written with Michael Anderle) – a post-apocalyptic paranormal adventure

Gateway to the Universe (co-written with Justin Sloan & Michael Anderle) – this book transitions the characters from the Terry Henry Walton Chronicles to The Bad Company

The Bad Company (co-written with Michael Anderle) – a military science fiction space opera

Judge, Jury, & Executioner (also available in audio) – a space opera adventure legal thriller

Shadow Vanguard – a Tom Dublin series

Superdreadnought (co-written with Tim Marquitz)– an AI military space opera

Metal Legion (co-written with Caleb Wachter) (coming in audio) – a military space opera

The Free Trader – a young adult science fiction action adventure

Cygnus Space Opera (also available in audio) – A young adult space opera (set in the Free Trader universe)

Darklanding (co-written with Scott Moon) (also available in audio) – a space western

Mystically Engineered (co-written with Valerie Emerson) – Mystics, dragons, & spaceships

End Times Alaska (also available in audio) – a Permuted Press publication – a post-apocalyptic survivalist adventure

Nightwalker (a Frank Roderus series) with Craig Martelle – A post-apocalyptic western adventure

End Days (co-written with E.E. Isherwood) (coming in audio) – a post-apocalyptic adventure

Successful Indie Author – a non-fiction series to help self-published authors

Metamorphosis Alpha – stories from the world's first science fiction RPG

The Expanding Universe – science fiction anthologies

Monster Case Files (co-written with Kathryn Hearst) – A Warner twins mystery adventure

Rick Banik (also available in audio) – Spy & terrorism action adventure

Published exclusively by Craig Martelle, Inc

The Dragon's Call by Angelique Anderson & Craig A. Price, Jr. – an epic fantasy quest

For a complete list of Craig's books, stop by his website – https://craigmartelle.com

www.ingramcontent.com/pod-product-compliance
Lightning Source LLC
Chambersburg PA
CBHW050152110726
47898CB00008B/2765